# Groups Welcome

## ETERNAL REST
### BED AND BREAKFAST

PARANORMAL COZY MYSTERIES

# BETH DOLGNER

Groups Welcome
*Eternal Rest Bed and Breakfast Book Six*
© 2022 Beth Dolgner

ISBN-13: 978-1-958587-01-0

Published by Redglare Press
Cover by Dark Mojo Designs
Print Formatting by The Madd Formatter

BethDolgner.com

Emily leaned forward, one hand shielding her eyes from the late-afternoon sun. "Scott, please..." she murmured.

The sounds around the bench where Emily sat seemed to fade as she focused all her attention on connecting with Scott. Every day for the past week, she had been sitting on the westward side of the hill that historic Hilltop Cemetery was built on. She spent as much time there as she could spare, trying to sense the presence of her late husband and hoping to catch a glimpse of his bright-green eyes.

Every day, she had walked home, disappointed.

Today felt different. The air seemed charged, as if something were coming. Emily could even feel the delicate hairs on the back of her neck rising. The sweltering summer weather felt more oppressive than usual, and Emily had the odd sensation that the air around her was being stretched like a rubber band, and it was almost at the breaking point. When that happened, there was going to be a snap in the form of some energetic force or paranormal activity.

Something was going to happen. Emily just didn't know what.

As the minutes wore on, Emily put her elbows on her knees and rested her chin in her hands. There was nothing to see in the hazy sky above the treetops that marched away in front of her, but she couldn't pull her eyes away. The anticipation was almost hypnotic.

"Scott, can you feel this energy, too?" Emily asked. Her voice seemed unnaturally loud, and when she spoke again, it was barely above a whisper. "Can you use this energy to communicate with me? I just want a sign that you're there. Please."

Only silence answered.

*It's too silent. I can't even hear the oak leaves rustling anymore.*

Fear flared through Emily as she remembered the last time nature had fallen silent around her. Even as she sat up and began to bring her hands in front of her face, palms out to ward off what she suddenly knew was coming, a black wisp, like distant smoke, shot up through the sky beyond the cemetery.

The smoke expanded, widening as it rushed toward Emily, then sharply contracted until it took on a dark, nearly opaque human shape. It lunged toward Emily, and even though it was still far away, somewhere well outside the wall of the cemetery, Emily pushed herself backward, her spine slamming into the back of the wooden bench. She turned her face away and shut her eyes.

An icy breeze sliced through the air around her, there and then gone just as quickly.

When nothing else happened, Emily lowered her hands slightly and opened her eyes.

The shadow was gone.

So was that feeling something was about to happen. The rubber band had snapped.

The wind—not icy this time, but the hot, humid air of North Georgia in July—again tickled the leaves in the oak trees, the sound soothing Emily as she took deep breaths and felt the adrenaline that was coursing through her begin to subside. A bird called from somewhere to her left, and a car rumbled along the two-lane road that led past the cemetery.

Emily's fear was mingled with disappointment that she had once again failed to get a sign from Scott. Her ghosts at Eternal Rest Bed and Breakfast had seen him, and her best friend had sensed him, yet Emily had only glimpsed Scott's ghost one time. It didn't seem fair.

With one last deep breath, Emily turned her head to gaze at the headstones on either side of her. "I'm safe," she told herself gently. "It can't hurt me here." The familiar monuments helped calm her, even as she reached up a shaky hand to run nervous fingers through her light-brown ponytail.

As Emily studied the inscription on the headstone to her left—a sentimental tribute to a man who had died in 1891—she heard someone approaching from her right, firm footfalls on the brick walkway. Emily's head swiveled around. Even while some little part of her brain shouted that perhaps the entity could, in fact, come into the cemetery, she recognized Detective Danny Hernandez walking toward her. His expression was a mixture of curiosity and concern, and when he came to a stop in front of Emily, he peered searchingly at her with his brown eyes.

"Did I scare you?" he asked.

"No," Emily assured him. "What brings you out here today, Danny?"

"I went to the house, and you weren't there. Since I know you have guests every night, I knew you couldn't be far away, so I thought I'd look for you here." Danny sat down on the bench next to Emily, his shoulder grazing hers. "Are you sure you're all right? You look... Well, I hate to say it, but you look like you just saw a ghost."

Emily gave a short laugh and nodded. "That's because I did just see a ghost."

Danny frowned. "You live with a houseful of them.

You're not easily scared by ghosts, so what did this one do?"

Emily gestured toward the treetops in front of them. "It lunged at me. I knew it couldn't reach me because it's not able to come through the psychic barrier that surrounds Oak Hill, but it was still scary." Emily brought her fingertips up to her cheek. "I felt the cold coming off it, though. Just a little bit, as if some part of it actually came through the barrier."

Danny gazed toward the horizon. "Sage told me about the barrier. She thinks it's weakening."

"Sage and I encountered this ghost twice before, when we were outside the barrier, and she wanted nothing to do with it. Honestly, I'm not even sure it is a ghost. It feels dark, almost evil, as silly as that might sound."

"It doesn't sound silly at all. It could be demonic."

Emily almost laughed, but she stopped herself when she saw how serious Danny looked. "Do you think demons are real?" she asked, trying to keep her tone neutral.

Apparently, her attempt didn't work, because Danny answered, "Really? You, haunted bed and breakfast hostess extraordinaire, are skeptical about demons?"

Emily shook her head slightly. "I know ghosts are real, but I've never experienced anything—well, other than this entity—that seemed evil or, as you say, demonic."

Danny looked at Emily thoughtfully. "I've never thought about it before, but Oak Hill really doesn't have any stories about truly scary or dangerous paranormal activity. Our ghosts are surprisingly well behaved."

"It's the psychic barrier, I suppose. If it's keeping this one entity out, then who knows what else it's barring from coming into town?" Emily shivered, despite the heat, and ran her hands briskly along her thighs, enjoying the feel of her sun-warmed black jeans against her palms.

Danny put a hand over one of Emily's, his fingers

squeezing hers softly. "I'm glad the barrier is here since it's keeping you safe," he said quietly, "but I'm worried what will happen if it continues to weaken. You know I don't like to see you in danger, Emily."

Suddenly, Emily's fear of the entity turned into fear that Danny had come to flirt with her. Quickly, she asked again, "What brings you out here today?"

"I was just coming to check on you. How's your head?"

"The lump on the back of my skull is gone, but I think it will take a while to recover from Allen Gerson threatening to kill me and my friends. It's only been a little more than a week, and I don't think the bad dreams about it are going to stop anytime soon."

Danny leaned closer to Emily, and his voice was soft when he spoke again. "Is that why you're out here? You're trying to sort through all of it?" His fingers tightened around hers.

*Doesn't he know I don't date?*

"I'm out here trying to make contact with Scott."

Danny's eyebrows drew together. "Scott?" Emily could hear his confusion.

"My late husband."

Danny muttered a surprised "oh" and sat up straight, immediately drawing his hand back from Emily's. "You mean you're trying to communicate with his ghost?"

"Exactly. Scott is somewhere just outside the barrier, but that dark entity is keeping him weak for some reason, so he can't come through. Sage and I are trying to figure out how to help him."

Emily could see the way Danny's cheeks flushed as he stammered, "I, I didn't know, Emily. I mean, I knew you'd lost your husband, but I had no idea his ghost... I'm so sorry."

Emily instinctively knew Danny was apologizing for showing his interest in her, rather than conveying sympathy about Scott's situation. If the two of them hadn't been interrupted the last time Danny had been looking at Emily with more than a friendly eye, maybe she would have told him then.

Feeling her own blush rising in her face, Emily said shyly, "Danny, I think you're great, but I'm not ready for, ah, getting back out there. Scott died two—almost three years ago now, and I've spent the entire time convinced his death wasn't an accident and wondering why his ghost wasn't around to tell me what really happened. Now, his ghost is finally here, but he's in trouble. I have to help him."

"You haven't let go yet," Danny said kindly, nodding, "because he's not really gone. If you think his death wasn't an accident, then why haven't you told me about it? I could help you track down the truth."

Emily smiled sadly at Danny. "That's sweet of you, but your detective work can't help in this case. I think it was something paranormal that killed him, maybe even that dark entity." Haltingly, Emily poured out her entire story to Danny. He had been such a big presence in her life lately that it had never occurred to her he didn't know about Scott's ghost. Somehow, though, he had never been there when the conversation had been about Emily's late husband.

When Emily was finished talking, Danny silently wrapped his arms around her, pulling her into a tight hug. Emily didn't feel any fear that this was a romantic gesture. She could feel the friendship and compassion in Danny's embrace, and she sighed in relief as she hugged him back.

It was a little after six o'clock by the time Emily said goodbye to Danny. She stood at the foot of her porch steps and waved as he drove away in his pickup truck. When Emily turned around to face her dark-blue Victorian clapboard house, she saw several bags and boxes sitting in front of the door. She had been in the cemetery so long she'd missed her friend Trish dropping off baked goods from Grainy Day Bakery. Now that Emily had the breakfast items for the next day, all she lacked was her guests, who had told her they would arrive early in the evening.

As Emily took the baked goods down the hall to the kitchen, she reflected on everything that had happened at the cemetery. She didn't doubt Danny was still interested in her romantically, but at least he knew now that all Emily wanted at the moment was a friend.

Emily was about to call Sage to fill her in on her brush with the entity when the doorbell rang. As she walked to the front door, Emily smoothed her button-down shirt and lamented how sticky she felt after being outside for so long. She opened the door, a smile already on her face, and saw two women who couldn't have looked more different.

The one who was short and plump reached out a hand and said crisply, "I'm Helen Harper. I'm the coven leader." Helen had sharp green eyes and a pinched mouth, and as Emily shook her hand, she wondered if Helen was annoyed or if she just looked that way.

"Welcome to Eternal Rest Bed and Breakfast," Emily said, shaking Helen's hand. "I'm looking forward to hosting your coven here this weekend." In reality, Emily had no idea what to expect. She had welcomed a few guests over the years who had called themselves witches, but she had never had an entire coven of them.

Emily turned to the second woman, who was so tall and thin Emily instantly thought of a supermodel. Amber-colored eyes gazed at Emily proudly above high cheekbones, and the woman's black hair cascaded in thick waves over her shoulders. "Kenyan and Brazilian," she said in a rich, slightly accented voice.

"I'm sorry?" Emily asked, confused.

"My heritage. You were standing there thinking how beautiful I am. It's not witchcraft, just good genes. I'm Abbie Morais."

"Nice to meet you, Abbie." Emily felt flustered by Abbie's looks and directness, but she tried to appear composed as she ushered the two women inside.

Emily gave Helen and Abbie their keys and told them where to find their rooms. The two women had just reached the upstairs landing when the doorbell rang again. Wondering if this next guest would be as interesting as the first two, Emily opened the door, telling herself to be ready for anything.

The woman standing there looked perfectly normal. In fact, she was average in almost every way, from her simple blue dress to her short graying hair. The only remarkable thing about her looks were her bright-green eyes.

Emily stared at her, too surprised to speak.

It was Darlene Buchanan, Scott's mother.

2

Emily stared at Darlene as her mind began to come up with reasons why her mother-in-law was standing on her doorstep. Darlene lived only a few hours away, and although they still talked on the phone regularly, Emily hadn't seen her in months. Maybe there was an emergency. Maybe Darlene missed her and had decided to drop in.

*Maybe my mother-in-law is a witch.*

Darlene smiled, though it looked more like a grimace. "Hi, Emily. Surprise?"

Emily glanced over her shoulder, toward the staircase Helen and Abbie had just ascended, then back to Darlene. She pointed behind her. "You're with them?"

"I assume you mean the coven leadership. They're the ones staying with you this weekend. I'm staying at The Carmichael Hotel on the square downtown."

"So you're…" Emily couldn't even finish her sentence. It sounded too ridiculous.

"A witch, yes," Darlene supplied. "I have been for decades."

"Oh."

"I wanted to come here tonight and tell you in person, so you had some time to let it sink in before we begin our first ritual here tomorrow."

Emily was suddenly aware of how rude she was being

to Darlene. Deciding to be completely honest, she said, "I'm a little overwhelmed by this news. I've never really believed witches were real, so finding out that you're one is a little shocking." Emily opened her arms. "Still, it's great to see you."

Darlene's smile this time was more comfortable, and she embraced Emily warmly. When they parted, Emily said, "Would you like to come in?"

"No, let's sit out here. I've always loved the porch swing."

As the two women settled onto the swing, Emily asked quietly, "Did Scott know?"

"That I'm a witch? Goodness, no! Even his dad only had the vaguest idea—Lonnie always thought I belonged to some sort of women's club."

"Why do you keep it secret?"

Darlene laughed. "I keep it secret because of the expression on your face when you opened the door and saw me. I live in a small town, too, and you know how the gossip would fly if word got out that I'm a witch. Everyone would look at me the way you did just now."

Emily winked at Darlene. "They'd probably confiscate your broom."

"I wish flying were part of the package. It's a lot more low-key than that, though."

"What can you tell me about the rituals your coven is doing here this weekend? Helen assured me it was nothing harmful, but she didn't give me any details."

"We'll be doing rituals each night from Thursday through Saturday to raise energy. Three nights, a powerful number. Then, on Sunday night, we'll have our final ritual, and we'll be channeling all of the energy we've raised into it. I'd tell you more, honey, but Helen keeps reminding us to keep quiet about it. Unlike me, she tells everyone she meets that she's a witch, but when it comes to the magic she works, she prefers secrecy."

"Understood. And I don't fault you for keeping this secret from me, Darlene. I don't run around bragging that I communicate with ghosts. I get enough weird looks as it is."

Darlene tilted her head. "I know Eternal Rest is haunted, but I didn't know you communicated with them. I thought your friend Sage did that, since she's a psychic medium."

Emily chuckled. "I guess you're not the only one with a secret, then. I've started developing mediumship skills myself."

Briefly, Emily considered telling Darlene that Scott's spirit hadn't crossed over yet, but she didn't want to distress her. Once they found a way to help Scott break free from the entity keeping him stuck outside the barrier, then, maybe, Emily would tell her. She and Darlene might be sharing secrets with each other, but that was one Emily wasn't going to divulge just yet.

Darlene and Emily had moved on to talking about how busy Eternal Rest Bed and Breakfast had been that summer when a car turned into the circular driveway. The white minivan came to a stop in the parking area, and soon, a woman with long black hair hopped out of it.

"Malena is here!" Darlene said happily. "Helen is our coven leader, and Abbie is sort of her second in command. Malena Lopez is our archivist. She keeps the records of our meetings, the spells we've done, what seems to work for us and what doesn't, and so on. Such a wealth of knowledge!"

"How many of you are there?" Emily asked as she stood, preparing to greet Malena.

"Seven, of course. Another magical number. Serenity, our herbs expert, will be here at Eternal Rest. Piper and

Evelyne are staying at the same hotel as me, and we'll just carpool over tomorrow afternoon."

Malena had gotten close enough to recognize Darlene, and her brown eyes lit up. "Darling Darlene! It's so good to see you!" Malena glanced at Emily, and she sounded hesitant as she added, "I hope everything is going well?"

"Emily was surprised by my news, but she recovered well," Darlene said, stepping forward to give Malena a peck on the cheek. "Give me your suitcase; I'll take it up for you. Emily, what room will she be in?"

"Three, the one above my room." Emily turned her attention to her latest guest. "Come on in. Welcome to Eternal Rest."

As the three women walked inside, Helen's voice sounded loudly from the upstairs landing. "No, that's not how we do things!"

"Not how you do things, you mean!" Abbie's voice was just as loud. "I know you're coven leader, but you act more like a coven dictator sometimes. I have ideas, Helen. Things that could help all of us."

"Great. When you're coven leader, you can implement those ideas. In the meantime, what I say goes."

Abbie grumbled something too low for Emily to hear, and a moment later, both women came downstairs. Abbie was stomping down each stair angrily while Helen followed, her chin high and a defiant look on her face.

Malena followed Emily into the parlor on the right side of the hallway while Darlene waited to greet Helen and Abbie. "I wonder if all covens have so much drama?" Malena said under her breath. Emily didn't respond, unsure if the words had even been meant for her. She gave Malena her room key and told her she would have sweet tea waiting for her when she was ready.

Abbie, who had glided into the parlor, spoke up. "Our

leadership meeting will start just as soon as Serenity arrives. We'll have our tea then."

Helen and Darlene were still standing in the hallway, chatting. Helen's expression had relaxed by the time Emily left the parlor, and she was grateful Darlene was there to calm the woman down.

As Emily busied herself in the kitchen, preparing coffee for the next morning, she heard Darlene's voice from the doorway. "Serenity just pulled in, so that's my cue to head out. The ladies will want to have their meeting as soon as she's settled so they can get to bed. We've got a big weekend ahead of us."

Emily put down the coffee filter and gave Darlene another hug. "I'm glad you're here," she said. "The next time someone I love tells me they're a witch, I promise to react better."

Darlene laughed. "Says my daughter-in-law the medium. I'll see you tomorrow, honey."

Emily turned back to the coffee maker, her mind whirling. In the span of just a few hours, Danny had introduced the possibility of demons, and Darlene had confessed to being a witch. Emily could only shake her head. She was busy enough with her ghosts, and she wasn't sure she could handle any other supernatural beings.

With a sigh and a wish for no more surprises that day, Emily walked down the hallway to see Darlene going out the front door as another woman was coming in it. The two of them spoke briefly, and then Emily was face-to-face with her fourth and final guest of the weekend.

The young woman was petite, with a pointed face and wide blue eyes. Her hair was piled up on top of her head, golden curls spilling down over her ears. "Hello," she said in a high, slightly breathy voice. "I'm Serenity."

Emily returned the greeting, taking in Serenity's long, layered silk skirt and purple tank top. Several pendants, including a pentagram, hung from chains around her neck, and at least a dozen bangle bracelets marched up one arm.

*All the women here call themselves witches, but Serenity looks like she might actually be a fairy.*

"Oh, Serenity, you're here," Helen said, a note of distaste in her voice. Emily turned and saw her standing in the dining room doorway. "You're late, as usual."

"I had to stop on the way to gather wildflowers. If you gather them while you're on a journey, you'll always make it home safely." Serenity smiled at Helen, no trace of apology for her tardiness apparent.

"Well, you're here now, so let's start this meeting. We have a lot to discuss." Helen turned her attention to Emily. "We'll take that tea now, thank you." Without waiting for a response, Helen turned and went back into the dining room.

"I'll get your room key," Emily told Serenity. "You'll be in room number four, at the top of the stairs on your left." Feeling slightly sympathetic for her after Helen's comments, Emily added, "I'll take your bag up for you."

Serenity actually had two bags with her. One was a normal suitcase, and the other was an old-fashioned carpet bag. As she lugged it up the stairs, Emily wondered if Serenity had filled it with bowling balls. The handles strained under the weight.

Once Serenity's luggage was safely inside her room, Emily walked quietly down the stairs to the kitchen. She could hear her guests speaking in low voices. Once four glasses of sweet tea had been loaded onto a tray, Emily went into the dining room.

Helen had been talking as Emily entered, but she fell silent as soon as Emily crossed the threshold, and Emily wondered what secretive stuff Helen had been discussing that she didn't want her to overhear. As Emily began to place a glass in front of each woman, Malena said, "I'm sure Emily could give us some recommendations for where to have lunch tomorrow."

"I'd be happy to," Emily said.

"You can ask her tomorrow," Helen said firmly. "Tonight, we're discussing more important things."

As Emily began to leave the room, Helen added curtly, "And close the door, please."

*At least she said* please.

Emily returned the tray to the kitchen, feeling strangely at odds with her new guests. She didn't mind that they wanted to have a private meeting, but she wasn't used to a guest speaking to her like Helen did.

"Who does she think she is?" Emily said, pushing the tray onto its spot on the shelf with a little more force than she had intended.

Emily returned to the parlor and settled in at the rolltop desk in the back corner. Soon, she was lost in confirming online reservation requests that had come through while she had been in the cemetery, and she was able to stop thinking about Helen and wondering if her position of leadership in the coven had gone to her head.

It was the sound of knocking, several sharp sounds on the wall in front of her, that finally pulled Emily's attention away from her laptop. "Mrs. Thompson?" she asked.

There were five more knocks, all loud, from the ghost of Emily's former assistant. It sounded urgent to her ears.

"Can Kelly tell me what you're trying to communicate?" Emily asked.

One knock confirmed that the ghost of Kelly Stern could relay a message, so Emily rose and walked to the front of the parlor. She gazed out the floor-to-ceiling windows while she waited for Kelly to write a message on the blank sheet of paper sitting next to Emily's laptop. Kelly would never write if Emily was watching. Emily kept paper and pens in the dining room and her bedroom, too, but Kelly seemed to prefer the parlor for writing notes.

After a couple of minutes, Emily returned to her desk and saw Kelly's message, which was in capital letters: *SO MUCH ANGER!*

"I know," Emily agreed. "Helen and Abbie were bickering, Helen seems annoyed with Serenity, and Malena definitely doesn't like the drama. I don't think this is a happy little coven."

This time, Emily double-checked that the front door was locked while waiting for Kelly to write a response. When she looked at the paper again, Kelly had added, *MORE THAN THAT. BIG ANGER, LIKE I HAD. IT'S SCARY.*

# 3

Before her killer had been brought to justice, Kelly's anger had spurred her to attack Emily's friend and one-time assistant, Trevor Williams. If Kelly was sensing that level of anger among the witches, then it didn't bode well for the weekend ahead.

*It's like that rubber band feeling again. Emotions are stretching, and if my guests aren't careful, they're going to snap.*

"Thank you, ladies," Emily called to the empty parlor. "I'm not sure I can really do anything to keep the peace among the coven, but please let me know if you sense any tensions that are about to boil over."

Mrs. Thompson gave a firm knock, and Emily sat down at her desk once again. Not long after, she heard the dining room door open and the tread of her guests' feet on the stairs. They were going to bed, so Emily soon followed suit.

The next morning, Emily was arranging the trays of breakfast food on the sideboard in the dining room as Serenity floated through the doorway, her gauzy white dress swirling around her ankles. "Oh, how lovely!" she enthused. "Good morning, Emily. I hope you slept well. I sprinkled some lavender water on the front doorstep before I came in last night to give us all pleasant rest."

Emily hadn't slept particularly well, which was usual

for her since Scott had died, but she didn't want to tell Serenity her magic hadn't worked. "That was sweet of you," she said instead. "Please, help yourself."

Serenity picked up a plate and began to pile baked goods and cheese onto it. Malena came into the room, and as Emily wished her a good morning, she saw Serenity pick up a biscuit. She stared at it with something like wonder, then said, "This was made with love. I can feel its energy. Did you know these are magic biscuits, Emily?"

It was everything Emily could do to keep a straight face. *Well, calling them magic biscuits is better than calling them murder biscuits. Wait until I tell Trish about this!* Emily knew her friend would get a kick out of someone calling her biscuits magical, especially when they had so recently been used to kill someone.

Emily quickly made her exit from the dining room, still biting her lip to keep herself from laughing, and retreated into the parlor. Her guests had just gone back upstairs after eating breakfast when Emily heard her assistant—and Trish's son—Clint, walk through the front door. His steps went into the dining room before coming to the parlor, and when Emily turned, he had a cup of coffee in his hand.

"Isn't seventeen too young to be drinking coffee?" she asked teasingly.

"I'm also too young to be hanging out with so many ghosts. They might warp my innocent young mind," Clint returned smoothly, raising his coffee cup and giving Emily a sly smile. "You're on tent duty, today, right?"

"Yeah, the rental company should be here shortly, so I've got to show them where to set up. I have no idea why these witches need such a big tent when there are only seven of them. Whatever rituals they're doing must take up a lot of space!"

"Witches?"

Emily grinned at Clint. "Did I forget to tell you? You'd

better get through at least one cup of coffee before I fill you in! You want to be awake for this news."

Soon, Emily was standing in the grassy expanse between Eternal Rest and Hilltop Cemetery, directing four men from the tent rental company where to set up a big white tent that could easily have held thirty people. Emily felt like she was overseeing preparations for an outdoor wedding, not a small group of guests.

Helen had been very specific about the direction the tent should face, and Emily was relaying this to one of the men, telling him the four sides of the tent should be aligned to the cardinal directions and pointing out which way was north, when behind her she heard someone say, "Witches are so picky, aren't they?"

Emily was already laughing as she turned around to see Sage Clark, looking tired but amused, standing behind her. Sage was wearing a white T-shirt and a denim skirt, which was remarkably normal and subdued for her. Frowning, Emily said, "Are you okay?"

"Look!" Sage patted her short, pink hair, which usually stood up in spikes. Today, it was flat. "Even my hair is exhausted. It's getting worse, Em. I had to cancel all my appointments today. I hate doing that to my clients, but I just don't have the energy to communicate with spirits this morning."

Sage made a living helping people connect with their dead loved ones, and Emily knew closing Seeing Beyond for a day had to be disappointing for Sage: not only was she not able to help her clients, but she wouldn't be making any money, either.

"Maybe the witches can whip up something to restore your energy," Emily quipped.

Sage swept a hand in the direction of the cemetery. "I think my exhaustion is tied to the barrier. As it weakens, so do I. So many ghosts are traveling through it and making themselves at home in Oak Hill. This town is on its way to being the most haunted city in Georgia, if not the country. Normally, if I feel like ghosts are draining my energy, I can put up a psychic shield. Now, though, there are too many of them. I'm overwhelmed."

"You're right about the barrier weakening. I saw the dark entity yesterday, Sage. The one we first met at the boathouse on Lake Otto. It lunged at me, and even though it can't come through the barrier yet, I felt the cold that it generates."

"That's not good."

"Agreed."

"I'm going to spend the afternoon working on my shielding. I actually came by hoping to talk to your guests in case they have a method to suggest."

Emily narrowed her eyes and leaned slightly toward Sage, looking for some sign that she was joking. "Seriously? I always thought witches were just fairy tales and middle-aged women with big ambitions. I mean, they can't really work magic. They just sprinkle herbs around and talk about vibrations, or whatever."

Sage crossed her arms. "Emily, since when are you a skeptic?"

Emily suppressed the urge to roll her eyes. "Danny said the same thing yesterday when he brought up the subject of demons."

"Let's go sit on the porch. It's too hot to stand out here in the sun. Whew, no wonder your guests asked for a tent! If they're spending a lot of time outside this weekend, they'll need the shade." Sage turned and headed for the porch swing, and Emily followed eagerly, curious to know why Sage seemed to believe in witches.

Once they were sitting, Sage began, "You just said it yourself, Em: vibrations. What is a ghost?"

"A person's spirit or, sometimes, residual energy that

has left an imprint in a place." Emily paused, then nodded. "This is about energy, then."

"Exactly," Sage said, sounding like a wise teacher who was pleased with her pupil. "Magic—witchcraft—is just energy. There's nothing special about sage—the plant, I mean. Obviously, I'm very special." Sage stopped to chuckle at her own joke. "Yet we used sage to cleanse your house of negative energy after Knight-MacGinn's murder. The sage wasn't what mattered, but our belief that it mattered. Our intention, and the energy we put into saging your house, is what made the difference. Our positive energy versus the lingering negative energy of your previous guests."

"That makes sense," Emily agreed.

"Well, that's what witches do, too. They create these rituals and spells as ways to focus their energy and direct it toward whatever change they want to enact. Ghosts are energy, you and I are energy inside these bodies, and witches use energy. I think it's one of the reasons I can so easily communicate with ghosts. At the end of the day, they're not that different from us."

Emily gazed ahead, her eyes unfocused as she thought about all of her encounters with ghosts. Even the dark entity that had lunged at her was just a form of energy, she realized, albeit the concentrated, negative kind. "And the psychic barrier is just energy, which is slowly dissipating," she said, more to herself than to Sage.

"There you go." Sage leaned her head back, tilting her face upward. "I could nap here."

"You're welcome to stick around, if you like."

"No, once I talk to your guests, I'm going to head home and work on shielding myself. If Jen weren't at her grandma's in North Carolina this week, I'd make her do it, too. I don't want her vulnerable, either. Are there any of your guests in particular you think I should consult?"

Emily turned to Sage, her eyebrows raised dramatically. "You could wait for Scott's mom to show up and ask her."

"Oh, is she a part of this coven?" Sage asked, not sounding at all surprised by what Emily thought might be the bombshell of the decade. When Emily remarked on Sage's blasé response, Sage waved a hand airily. "Of course she's a witch. Did you not know? She wears those two amulets around her neck, and she has that quartz ring on her right hand."

"She always wears the same necklaces, yes," Emily agreed, "but I always thought she wore them simply because they were pretty."

Sage smiled. "They are pretty, but they're also warding symbols. The quartz ring is for spiritual protection, too. I learned about things like that when I was in college and looking for ways to keep myself safe from malicious ghosts. In the end, I went with the ankh instead, since it reminds me that ghosts are just people who parted ways with their bodies. We are eternal." Sage wrapped her fingers lovingly around the silver pendant that hung from a chain around her neck.

"How funny that the signs were there the whole time, and none of us close to her knew it. Darlene told me Scott and his dad were always in the dark about what she is."

Sage's tone was a lot more subdued when she said, "I wonder if Scott's situation has something to do with Darlene's witchcraft. The entity keeping him weak and bound to this plane might be getting revenge for magic she or her coven worked against it."

Emily pressed her lips together in a tight line. "I hate to think Darlene had anything to do with Scott's death. Although, Scott was driving home from her house when he crashed."

Sage and Emily both sat silent for a few moments, and eventually, Sage put her arm around Emily's shoulders.

"We don't know the truth yet, but you know as well as I do that Darlene would never intentionally put her son in danger. Does she know his ghost is nearby?"

Emily shook her head. "That's not a subject I know how to broach."

"She needs to know at some point. She deserves to know."

"You're right. If you're willing, I'd like you to be there when I tell her. I think I'll need the moral support."

"Of course." Sage gave Emily's shoulders a squeeze as the front door opened and Helen stalked out, followed closely by Abbie. Sage jumped up from the swing and said brightly, "Hello, witches! I'm Sage, and I need your help!"

Sage wound up staying at Eternal Rest much longer than Emily had expected. Helen and Abbie were open to assisting her, but Malena seemed especially eager. Emily removed the remains of breakfast while Sage and the witches settled in at the dining room table, and Malena was quick to note that having a psychic medium as a friend and colleague could be valuable for the coven.

Meanwhile, Emily made sure the tent was installed correctly and cleaned the guest rooms. By lunchtime, the tent and seven white plastic folding chairs were in place, Sage was heading home to work on some new shielding rituals, and Clint was on the phone, talking to someone who seemed to be asking about a Thanksgiving stay at Eternal Rest.

The witches had just moved outside—after Abbie had told Emily in an authoritative tone that fresh air and real earth underfoot were always preferable to being inside—when there was a knock on the front door.

Emily opened the door to see a woman who looked to be in her late fifties. She had short graying hair, and her bright turquoise scarf fluttered over a long black dress. She was looking to her right, toward the tent. "I'll be there in a minute!" she yelled, even though Emily didn't see anyone when she followed her gaze.

The woman turned her head toward Emily with a start. "Oh, hi. I'm Evelyne Grayson. I know I'm in the right place because I could sense Helen from one town over. 'Witch' is close to the right word for her, but it's off by one letter."

Emily's guests had a late lunch delivered on Thursday, and they chose to eat in the tent despite the heat of the afternoon. Emily wondered if it was really the fresh air and dirt they were after or the chance to speak without fear of being overheard by her.

While her guests ate, Emily ran to the store for a few items. Afterward, when she pulled into the driveway of Eternal Rest as looming storm clouds chased behind, she saw someone standing on her front doorstep. Even as she passed the front of the house to park in the back, the door began to open, and she knew Clint was greeting the newcomer.

By the time Emily had unloaded her shopping bags and plopped them down on the kitchen table, Clint was again the only other person in the house. He appeared in the kitchen, the cordless phone in one hand, and said bluntly, "This is a weird group of guests, Emily, and it's not just because they say they're witches."

Emily put a carton of eggs in the fridge and turned to face Clint. "What do you mean?"

Clint glanced toward the hallway, then took a step closer to Emily so he could speak quietly. "The woman who just arrived seemed angry. I don't have any special abilities like you and Sage, but in my sophomore year, we could always tell if our math teacher was having a bad day as soon as we walked into the classroom. This lady felt like that. She was perfectly polite, but she seemed kind of fed up."

*How does Darlene put up with these people?*

"There does seem to be a lot of tension among them," Emily agreed. As if to punctuate her point, a loud clap of thunder sounded just as the sunlight streaming through the kitchen windows disappeared. "And it's going to storm, so we're about to have a full house," she added.

Within five minutes, Emily's prediction came true as the witches filed through the front door. Emily came out of the kitchen to check on them and was relieved they hadn't actually gotten caught in the rain. Most of them settled in the dining room, but Serenity headed upstairs, and Emily overheard her saying something about harnessing the power of the lightning while she mounted the steps. Emily hoped she meant it metaphorically and not literally.

A few minutes later, the woman Emily had seen at the front door came into the kitchen, knocking lightly against the doorframe as Emily turned toward her. The newcomer had on a lime-green polo shirt and a pair of white pants that looked like they had been tailored for her. Dark-blonde bangs framed a tan face. "Hello, you must be Emily. I'm Piper Carlson. Thank you for hosting our event this weekend."

As Emily shook Piper's hand, she understood why Clint had gotten such a strong negative impression of her. Piper sounded friendly enough, and she flashed a smile full of perfect white teeth, but there was some nagging undercurrent Emily couldn't quite pinpoint.

"Did you just get to town?" Emily asked politely.

"Yes. No point in staying away from home more nights than I need to. I live in Buckhead, so it's not too far of a drive." Piper raised a hand and gave her car keys a little shake before disappearing down the hallway. Emily wasn't surprised to see a Mercedes key chain. It seemed to fit with Piper's preppy style and the fact that she lived in a wealthy Atlanta neighborhood.

Emily had finished up her work in the kitchen and was putting dish towels away in the hall closet when Clint came racing out of the parlor. He rushed up to Emily, but instead of saying anything, he simply held up a sheet of white paper. Kelly's handwriting—the small, almost timid style she used when she was scared or upset—covered the entire sheet. She had written, over and over, *Can't breathe.*

Emily sidestepped Clint and hurried to the parlor. "Kelly?" she called. "Kelly, what's going on? Are you okay? What do you mean, you can't breathe?" Kelly had once sent Emily visions of her murder through dreams, and Emily remembered all too vividly the horror and panic of being choked to death.

Clint had followed Emily into the parlor, and after putting a fresh sheet of paper next to her laptop, she took him by the arm and steered him toward the front windows. "Let's give her a couple of minutes to write."

"What do you mean?" Clint glanced over his shoulder toward the desk.

"She won't write if we're looking."

Clint shook his head. "No, I saw it, Emily. I had gotten up to ask our guests if they needed anything, and when I came back in here, the pen was moving across the paper by itself."

Even amid her worry for Kelly, Emily still felt a slight pang of envy that Clint had actually seen Kelly's ghost in the act of writing a message. Struck with a sudden idea, she said, "You know, you should talk to her when you're here. Talk about school or football, anything you want. She was only seventeen when she died. Kelly might like having a friend the same age as her."

"I'll try," Clint said, though he looked slightly unsure about the idea.

Emily returned to her desk, and Kelly had written, *So much anger. So much unhappiness. Can't breathe.*

Emily sighed. "It sounds like she's getting the same impressions from these guests as you and me," she told Clint. "Mrs. Thompson, Kelly is feeling overwhelmed by our guests. Can you please reassure her that she's safe?"

"Who is Kelly, and how are we overwhelming her?" someone asked from behind Emily. She recognized Darlene's voice.

"Kelly is a ghost here," Emily said, facing Darlene. "She's very sensitive to the emotions of others."

Darlene nodded. "This coven does travel with a lot of baggage. It wasn't always like this, and I expect things will eventually calm down, once we've gotten some egos under control. In the meantime, you can tell your ghost she's got nothing to worry about." Darlene smiled as she turned her eyes toward the empty air above her.

Emily considered telling her that Kelly wasn't the only ghost she was trying to help. She wanted to know if Scott's situation really might be tied to Darlene's witchcraft, as Sage had speculated, but Emily still couldn't force her mouth to form the words. It was just too difficult and delicate of a thing for her to talk about with a woman who had no idea her son was a ghost.

The storm only lasted a short while, like so many of the afternoon thunderstorms that rolled through Georgia in the summer. The sunlight soon streamed in through the windows again as the final echoes of thunder faded away. When Emily went outside to retrieve the mail, the air felt even thicker than usual, so she wasn't surprised when her guests declared they would stay indoors for a while.

*I guess that whole fresh air and earth underfoot attitude has its limits.*

The rest of the afternoon passed slowly for Emily. She tried to keep quiet so she wouldn't disturb her guests, and since Clint was there to handle phone calls and book reservations, there wasn't much for her to do. Finally realizing she may as well take care of some boring but necessary tasks, Emily sat down at the kitchen table with her little sewing basket and a few throw pillows whose stitching had started to unravel.

While she worked, Trish texted to say she would be late delivering the baked goods for Friday morning's breakfast, so Emily didn't even have that to look forward to until at least dinnertime. After she finished stitching up the pillows, she moved on to cleaning up a few old, ornate frames she had found in the attic. They would look great in the hallway when paired with vintage photos of the house.

At five o'clock, Emily went to the parlor to relieve Clint. She had expected him to be grateful to be done for the day, but instead he said haltingly, "I thought maybe I could stay a little late and help you with some things around the house."

"Like what?"

"Well… Your social media feeds aren't very up to date. I can help with that."

Emily crossed her arms. "I'd love for you to help with that, but why does it have to be tonight? Do you not want to go home for some reason?"

"It's just…" Clint dropped his gaze to the floor, and he shifted awkwardly from one foot to the other. He cleared his throat and said shyly, "Kelly and I are getting to know each other."

"Oh, Clint, that's great! What kinds of things has she been writing? Is she feeling a little better?"

Even though he was still avoiding looking directly at her, Emily could see the way Clint's cheeks flushed. "I guess. We've been talking about our favorite movies and bands, and stuff like that."

*I think Clint is flirting with my ghost.* Emily didn't know whether she should laugh or be concerned. Still, if it helped Kelly calm down, then she wasn't against it, as long as Clint didn't get too attached to her. Gently, Emily reminded Clint that Kelly would still be there next Tuesday, when he would be back at Eternal Rest to work. She added that she would be happy to pass along any messages Kelly might leave for him in the meantime.

After Clint reluctantly left for the evening, Emily's curiosity got the better of her, and she went to her desk to see what kinds of things Kelly had written to Clint. There was only a blank sheet of paper on the desk. Clint had taken the conversation home with him.

At six o'clock, Helen came into the parlor and told Emily she and the rest of the coven were driving into downtown Oak Hill to eat dinner. "We have to build up our strength for our ritual tonight," Helen said seriously.

Once they were gone, the house was blissfully quiet. The witches might have come to Eternal Rest to raise energy, but Emily felt like they were draining hers. "You're going to have a couple hours of peace and quiet, Kelly," Emily announced to the empty house.

Emily used the time to make her own dinner and to relax for a few moments with a book. All too soon, the witches were back, though Emily's disappointment didn't last long. She heard them treading up the stairs, then back down again. The front door shut with a bang, and the house was quiet again. Emily assumed they were heading to the tent to conduct their first energy-raising ritual.

No sooner had Emily settled in with her book again than the doorbell rang. As she had expected, it was Trish. "Long day?" Emily asked as she plucked the bags and boxes of baked goods out of Trish's hands. Trish was looking to her right, though, and she didn't seem to hear Emily.

"The tent is for my guests," Emily explained, assuming that was what had caught Trish's attention.

Trish wrapped her fingers around the end of her long blonde French braid and started twisting it nervously. "Emily," she said slowly in her thick Southern accent, "what are your guests doing?"

"Conducting some kind of ritual."

"No, they're not. Look." Trish pointed toward the cemetery with her free hand. Emily stepped onto the front porch and looked in the direction of Hilltop Cemetery. The witches were climbing over the low stone wall that surrounded it.

Emily sighed in exasperation. "They didn't ask for permission to go in there. It can be dangerous at night, especially without flashlights. If they had just asked, I would have unlocked the gate for them and made sure they took precautions."

Even as she watched, Piper awkwardly scrambled over the top of the wall. Her white pants stood out like a beacon in the near darkness, and she was wiping the back of them aggressively.

"That lady did not dress for climbing walls," Trish noted.

"If you hear sirens later, it's just an ambulance coming for a broken ankle. Or maybe they cast a spell so they won't fall in a hole or trip over a tree root." Emily couldn't keep the sarcasm out of her voice.

"Good luck," Trish said with a snicker. "And good night!"

Emily stood and gazed at the cemetery until all the women had faded into the gloom. Realizing she still had the baked goods in her arms, Emily just shook her head and went inside.

Half an hour later, Emily was once again sitting with her book, this time in the parlor. The coffee maker was prepped for the next morning, and all she had to do at the moment was wait for her guests to return so she could go to bed.

Several knocks sounded in quick succession, and initially, Emily thought someone was knocking on the door. As she stood, though, she heard more rapid knocks and realized they were coming from the back wall of the parlor.

"Mrs. Thompson? What's wrong?" Emily asked.

The knocking just increased, both in frequency and volume, and Emily knew her one-time assistant was agitated about something. "Kelly, can you please write down why Mrs. Thompson is so upset?"

Before she could even give Kelly time to write, Emily heard a scream from outside, followed by many hurried footsteps on her front porch. The front door banged open as Emily reached the hallway, and she saw Abbie standing there, the other witches crowded together behind her.

"She's dead!" Abbie said, her voice cracking. "Helen is dead!"

5

Someone at the back of the group was still moving forward, and they set off a chain reaction that propelled Darlene over the threshold and into Malena's shoulder, which sent Malena flying toward Abbie. Instinctively, Emily reached toward Abbie as she stumbled, but she regained her balance, throwing a scathing look over her shoulder before straightening up to her full height.

Thoughts flitted through Emily's mind while the crush of bodies regrouped in the hallway. *And here I thought it would just be a sprained ankle. I should have followed them out there so this couldn't happen. Am I going to get sued because someone died on my property?*

Emily took a deep breath to calm her racing mind and heart, and she said as calmly as she could, "Are you sure Helen isn't just injured?"

"I was a nurse when I was younger," Evelyne said, managing to sound both haughty and hysterical at the same time. "I know the difference between just injured and dead. There was no pulse, and I couldn't detect any breathing. She was... There was no point in trying CPR."

After that, things happened in a blur. Emily suddenly found herself with the phone up to her ear, waiting on a nine one one dispatcher to answer. She felt like she had switched into some kind of robotic mode, mechanically going through the right steps without really absorbing what she was doing or the fact one of her guests had just died.

The witches were crying, clutching each other's hands as they stood there in the hallway. Emily had to retreat to the parlor to talk to the dispatcher. Once the conversation was over, she lowered the phone but stayed standing exactly where she was. Her eyes were fixed on a painting of Eternal Rest that hung above her desk, but she wasn't really seeing it.

Emily wasn't sure how long she stood there like that, but it was the sound of a siren that finally snapped her into action again. She pushed her way through the witches as gently as she could and hurried out the front door and down the porch steps. The ambulance was just pulling into her driveway, and she walked toward it as it came to a stop and two EMTs alighted.

"Ma'am, where was the accident?" one of them, a young woman with brown hair pulled back in a tight bun, asked.

"In the cemetery," Emily said, her voice seeming to come from far away, as if it were someone else's. She looked up when she saw a blue flash, and she realized a police car was pulling in behind the ambulance.

"Can you show us the exact spot?" the woman continued.

Emily blinked. "No, actually. I'm not sure where it happened or, for that matter, how it happened. My guests were the ones who found her. Hang on." Emily turned and jogged back to the house. The front door was standing wide open, so she stayed on the porch and called Abbie's name loudly. Since Abbie was the one who had told her the news, Emily decided she should be the one to lead them to Helen's body.

Instead of just Abbie, all six women trooped out of the house, and they moved in a tight cluster down the porch

34

steps. Emily turned and began walking toward the cemetery gate, pulling her keys out of her pocket while silently reproaching herself for not grabbing a flashlight, too. Suddenly, the way ahead of her lit up, and she looked over, startled to realize Roger Newton had fallen into step beside her. Luckily, he and the EMTs all had flashlights.

Emily felt some relief to have Officer Newton by her side. His presence felt comforting, and she knew that no matter what they found in the cemetery, he would be right there with her.

Soon, Abbie was leading the way up the brick walkway that led straight from the ornate iron gate of Hilltop Cemetery to the crest of the hill. When Abbie spoke, she seemed to have recovered some of her composure. "I found her on the far side of the hill, in the southwestern area." She pointed ahead and slightly to her left.

Abbie walked quickly on her long legs, and as the rest of them tried to keep up, Emily could see she wasn't the only one who was out of breath by the time they reached the top of the hill. Darlene and Evelyne were both trailing slightly behind the group. Abbie finally slowed her pace as she went down the far side of the hill a short distance and stepped off the path onto the grass, weaving her way carefully between headstones. She began directing one of the EMTs where to shine his flashlight, and soon, Abbie pointed and said, "There she is."

It was only in that moment Emily realized she should have stayed at the very back of the group, or even in the house, so she didn't have to see Helen's body. Before she could avert her eyes, though, it was right there, spotlighted in the flashlight's beam. From her angle, Emily realized, Helen looked like she was simply asleep. She was on her side, her back to the onlookers and her face turned toward a headstone with a cherub statue atop it.

Abbie began narrating her story, her hands flying as

she gestured dramatically toward Helen. "We split up so we could raise our energy across a wider stretch of the circle, and we had reached a point in our ritual where we were repeating lines of an incantation, one after the other. Serenity, on my left, said it, then it was my turn, and Helen should have been next. She was silent, though, and she didn't answer when I called out to her. I went to see if anything was wrong, and I found her like this."

The EMTs and Roger all moved forward, and Emily heard the woman say, "Looks like she hit her head on the edge of this tombstone. She must have tripped and fallen."

Emily pressed her lips into a thin line, again berating herself for not chasing after the witches and insisting they use flashlights and a healthy dose of caution inside the cemetery.

Roger's voice rose above the din of the witches, whose crying had increased the second they saw Helen's prone form again. "Ladies, please!" he said, politely but firmly. "We need you all to return to the house. Please, stay there."

It was Serenity who roused her coven, saying soothing things in a choked tone while holding out her arms and herding the witches in the direction of the house. Darlene joined the effort, and the group moved off slowly, with Emily's warning for them to stay on the pathway and to mind their steps trailing after them.

"You don't need to stay here, either, Miss Emily," Roger added.

Emily was tempted to tell Roger she would prefer to stay there in the cemetery, and that being around a dead body might be better than being around the crying, upset witches. Instead, she said, "Okay, but let me know if you need any help."

Roger strode forward, closing the gap between himself and Emily. His close-cropped blond hair seemed to glimmer in the moonlight, and he narrowed his eyes to peer at Emily. "Do you think this death was intentional?"

Emily was on the verge of saying no, of course it was just an accident, but then, her thoughts returned to the notes Kelly had been writing. Kelly was feeling overwhelmed by the anger and emotion she felt radiating off the witches. It was so bad that even Clint, whom Emily doubted had any kind of psychic abilities, could sense it.

Not only did Emily not want to believe Helen's death was tied to those things, but she knew Roger would never believe it. She could picture the exact look he would give her if she told him one of her ghosts had gotten a bad feeling from this coven.

"They all seem very upset," Emily finally said lamely. "When I saw them hopping the fence to come in here, I even worried someone would get hurt. I just never imagined someone would get a fatal injury."

"All right. Go make yourself and your guests some hot tea, and try to calm them down, if you can. I know this is hard for them to lose a friend so unexpectedly."

Emily could hear the sympathy in Roger's voice. She thanked him and promised there would be fresh coffee at the house if he or the EMTs wanted it, then walked slowly and thoughtfully back to the house.

The witches had taken over the parlor. Malena, Serenity, and Piper were squeezed together on the antique sofa that faced the front windows. Abbie sat regally, her face composed and her back straight, in one of the wingback chairs while Evelyne sat in the other, dabbing at her cheeks with a handkerchief. Darlene was pacing back and forth in front of Emily's desk, her lips moving softly, and her eyes focused on the wooden floor.

"What are we going to do?" Piper asked, her voice shaking.

"We're going to continue, of course," Evelyne said.

"We can't do these rituals without a coven leader!" Piper looked horrified at the idea.

"Of course we can," Malena said. "We don't have the power of seven now, but we can still raise energy. We can still work the magic we came here to work."

"I don't know," Darlene said, still pacing and staring at the floor. "It seems like forces are working against us."

"Helen had an unfortunate accident," Evelyne countered. Emily noted that Evelyne didn't sound like she really found it all that unfortunate. Her tone was matter of fact. "We have to continue. You know that, Darlene."

"I know, I know." Darlene fell silent again, her lips still forming words.

Emily, standing in the parlor doorway, felt a wave of sadness. Despite the anger and drama in this group, they were still close to one another, and she suspected being in a coven wasn't all that different than being in a family. Everyone may not get along all the time, but at the end of the day, they shared a special bond.

Without asking the witches whether they wanted it or not, Emily took Roger's advice and went to the kitchen to make a pot of tea. She piled teacups, milk, sugar, and spoons onto a tray. Once the kettle got the water boiling, she poured it into the pot with a generous amount of dried chamomile and added it to the tray, too. Maybe, Emily hoped, it would help calm everyone a bit.

Once the tea was ready, Emily returned to the parlor and began passing out cups. A few of the women thanked her quietly, and all of them gratefully accepted the tea. Emily was just filling Darlene's cup when there was a knock on the front door.

Emily put down the teapot and walked to the door with a rising feeling of dread. Hearing several sharp knocks on the hallway wall only added to her worry. Mrs. Thompson was still upset about something.

*Or, maybe,* Emily thought, her hand already on the doorknob, *it's a warning.*

It was Roger at the door, and Emily knew from the set of his jaw that her apprehension had been justified. "Miss Emily, can I please talk to you outside?" he asked quietly.

Emily shut the door behind her and was surprised to see that Roger was walking off the porch. Clearly, he didn't want any chance of being overheard. When he was halfway to his patrol car, he finally stopped and faced Emily.

"The victim's death wasn't an accident," Roger began. "Maybe she did fall and hit her head, but not before someone stabbed her in the chest. I'm sorry, Miss Emily, but your cemetery is now a crime scene."

# 6

Emily glanced over her shoulder at the house. Someone had thrown open the parlor curtains, despite the fact it was dark outside, and the warm light spilling out of them gave Eternal Rest a welcoming glow.

*Too bad there might be a murderer in there.*

Emily returned her attention to Roger. "Do you think one of the witches did this? Or, maybe someone was hiding in the cemetery, waiting for Helen, and they ran off before they got caught."

"Did you notice if one of your guests was carrying a knife when they went to the cemetery?" Roger asked. The grim set of his mouth told Emily he did, indeed, believe one of the witches had killed Helen.

"No, I didn't." Struck with another thought, Emily suddenly said, "Evelyne examined the body! She told me she used to be a nurse. She said Helen wasn't breathing, but there was no point in trying CPR. Do you think she noticed the stab wound? And if she did, why didn't she tell me? Did she tell the other witches?"

Roger lifted a hand to his face, and Emily heard a quiet snort. He was trying to suppress laughter.

"What?" Emily asked self-consciously.

"You, already diving into the investigation. Are you

sure running a B and B is what you want to do with your life? You'd look nice with a badge, Miss Emily."

Emily couldn't find it in her to see any humor in the situation, but she did get Roger's point. "I know, I should leave this to the professionals."

"That information about one of your guests examining the victim is interesting, though." Roger pulled a pen and a small notepad out of his pocket and began writing. "What did you say her name is?"

"Evelyne. She's not staying here, though. Four of the witches are staying with me, and three of them are staying at The Carmichael."

"Witches," Roger muttered under his breath, shaking his head in disapproval. Emily suspected he was as skeptical about witches as he was about ghosts. At least, when it came to witches, she shared his opinion. Despite everything Sage had said about witchcraft just being another way to work with energy, Emily was still having a hard time believing her guests were able to really do anything.

Roger made a few more notes, then looked up at Emily. "I'll start talking to them right away. I'd like to get their stories while it's all fresh in their minds."

"Okay. I'll keep making coffee until you've gotten through all of them." Headlights suddenly blared in Emily's face, and she looked up to see a car pulling into the driveway. As it got closer, she saw it wasn't a car at all, but a pickup truck. Detective Danny Hernandez was on the case.

Danny parked behind Roger's patrol car and nearly sprinted over to Emily. He grabbed her hand and held it tightly while giving her a searching look. "Are you okay?"

"Oh, sure. I've got another murder victim in my cemetery, and this one is a lot more recent than Kelly Stern." Emily's voice was deadpan, and she realized how heartless her response sounded. She gave Danny's hand as much of a squeeze as she could when he was already holding hers so tightly. "Sorry. I'm just feeling a little overwhelmed by it all. I hate that this happened."

"We'll get through it," Danny said with a nod. Suddenly, he let go of Emily's hand and glanced away. His eyes met Roger's, and he simply said, "Shall we?"

"Do you want to take a statement from the Wicked Witch of the West or the good one in the poofy dress?" Roger asked.

"Roger," Emily began hesitantly, "I mean, Officer Newton."

"Roger is fine."

"Okay. Well, uh, you should know… You should both know…" Why was sharing this piece of news so hard for Emily? Was she embarrassed to be so closely tied to a witch? "Scott's mother is in there. She's a member of this coven."

"Scott was your husband, right? Interesting," Roger said. He sounded surprised, but there was also a note of suspicion in his voice when he said, "Is that how you talk to your ghosts, Miss Emily? You cast a spell or something?"

Emily shook her head. "No. I didn't even know Darlene was a witch until she showed up here last night." Emily almost went on to say she didn't need any kind of magic or spells to communicate with the ghosts of Eternal Rest, but she stopped herself just in time. She hoped Roger would someday become a believer, but she doubted this was the night for it.

The witches were still in the parlor, and Emily called loudly to get their attention. As she introduced Danny and explained he and Roger were going to take everyone's statements, the only sounds were occasional sniffles from the witches, high-pitched moans from Serenity, and labored gasps from Malena, who eventually dug an asthma inhaler out of her pocket.

Sage called just as Danny was leading Evelyne into the dining room to take her statement, and Roger was heading toward the kitchen with Darlene behind him. Emily answered her phone with, "Is the rumor mill really that fast?"

"All I know is that an ambulance and a police car were seen parked outside Eternal Rest," Sage answered. "What's going on?"

Emily stepped out the front door so she could have some privacy and began pacing back and forth across the porch. She told Sage everything, the hand not holding the phone waving wildly as she described the chaos of the evening. All of the shock, stress, and sorrow of the past couple of hours were finally sinking in, and Emily was no longer feeling like a robot just going through the motions. She didn't have the emotional connection to Helen that the witches did, but still, one of her guests had been killed on her own property. The grim reality of the situation felt like a weight on her chest.

When her story was finally finished, Emily felt her knees buckle. She sank down onto the wooden boards of the porch, her back against a column and her legs stretched out in front of her. "What am I going to do, Sage?"

"Help solve the murder, obviously," Sage answered in a matter-of-fact tone. "You'll have to rely on your own psychic abilities more than mine, though. I'll do as much as I can, but this exhaustion is forcing me to limit my interaction with ghosts. Still, I'll come help, of course."

"Thanks. You know I appreciate it. Just having you here will help me feel less lost. I think the first thing we need to do is have a long chat with Kelly and Mrs. Thompson. Kelly has been really agitated by all the anger and negative emotions these witches are putting out, and Mrs. Thompson has been banging on the walls tonight like she has something urgent to communicate. I just need the police to leave and the witches to go to bed so I can have a little chat with them."

"I'm on my way."

"Sage, you just said you're exhausted!" Emily couldn't help feeling amused by her best friend's stubbornness. "I can muddle my way through the conversation tonight."

"I'm happy you're willing to try, Em, but this will go faster if I'm there." Sage paused, chuckled quietly, and added, "Plus, I confess I'm a little curious to be a fly on the wall at Eternal Rest right now. I might pick up on some feelings from those ladies that could be useful in finding out who killed Helen."

"I'm hoping Kelly will have an idea who's giving off the feelings of anger, too. That information could really help us narrow down our suspect list."

Emily still felt overwhelmed when she hung up, but she at least felt better knowing Sage was on her way. She stayed put on the porch, closing her eyes and tipping her head back to rest it against the porch column. The evening air was still warm, but the breeze was soothing, and Emily much preferred the noises of crickets and a distant owl to the sounds of six shocked and grieving women.

*Five shocked and grieving women,* Emily corrected herself. *One of them is only pretending to be upset by this.*

It wasn't until Emily heard the sound of a car in the driveway that she finally opened her eyes. She craned her neck around and recognized Sage's car. Wearily, Emily stood and went down the porch steps to meet her.

Sage caught Emily in a tight hug. "It's the summer of murder, isn't it?" Sage said lightly. "It hasn't even been two weeks since you helped catch Allen Gerson."

"It's been nine days," Emily said flatly.

"Let's go in so I can start getting some impressions. The sooner we sort this out, the sooner you can get back to normalcy." Sage walked right into the parlor, where she gave the assembled women her condolences. Emily followed but stayed closer to the doorway, feeling reluctant to rejoin the group.

Darlene and Evelyne had finished giving their statements, and Abbie said that Serenity had gone to the kitchen with Roger while Piper was being interviewed by Danny. Emily hoped Mrs. Thompson and Kelly were observing in the kitchen because she would love to know how Roger was reacting to Serenity. Emily imagined her sprinkling the room with herbs at that moment to ensure a smooth investigation.

For the next hour, Emily served coffee and tea while continuing to say sympathetic things to the coven. Sage had sat down on the couch and was talking easily with them, and it wasn't until the last two witches—Abbie and Malena—were being interviewed that Emily realized Sage's presence was actually good for the women. Her conversation was a distraction for them, and the mood in the parlor felt more calm than it had all night.

Finally, Danny and Roger returned to the parlor. Danny merely looked tired, but Roger shifted his gaze to the far wall and slowly rubbed a hand across the back of his neck. Emily walked up to them and said quietly, "What?"

"We need to talk to all of you," Roger said, his eyes still on the wall.

Emily stepped back as Danny asked for everyone's attention. "Ladies, I regret to inform you that until we know who is responsible for Ms. Harper's death, you are not allowed to return home. As of right now, you are all staying here at Eternal Rest for the duration of this investigation. You can go outside, but you are not to leave the property. We will have police officers stationed here to ensure you comply. Let's all hope this is swiftly resolved."

The six witches began talking at once. Abbie stood up angrily, but it was Evelyne's voice that cut through the din. "My belongings are at my hotel. Are you going to bring them to me?"

"We have officers coming to escort you there right now," Roger said. "You can pack up and return."

"I have to be back at work on Tuesday," Malena said.

"Then let's hope this murder is solved by then," Danny answered smoothly.

"Do you need to search Helen's room?" Emily asked. "If not, I can give one of the women staying at the hotel that room."

"We won't be searching it until tomorrow," Danny said. "Ms. Harper's room is off-limits until then."

"Of course." Emily was already thinking about the logistics of having six guests and only three guest rooms. Darlene could stay in her room, Emily figured, since having a king-sized bed meant she would hardly even notice Darlene was there. Room Four was actually two twin beds pushed together, so she could separate those. That just left one person who needed a place to sleep.

Serenity actually came to the rescue, announcing, "Someone can have my bed, as long as there are some extra blankets and pillows I can put on the floor for myself. I'll cast a deep-sleep spell, so I shouldn't even notice if it's uncomfortable."

Darlene, Evelyne, and Piper were taken to The Carmichael and then brought back, their luggage in tow. Officers were stationed at the front and back of the house by that time, so Roger and Danny wished everyone a good night and left. Finally, Sage and Emily were alone in the parlor.

Sage wasted no time getting in touch with Mrs. Thompson's ghost. "Mrs. Thompson, why were you so agitated earlier?"

Emily eagerly watched Sage, who occasionally nodded. Finally, Sage said, "Mm-hm, that makes sense. That's why you started knocking on the walls before the witches came and told Emily the news. Okay, see what you can find out for me, and tell her we're working on it. I need to go home and rest, but I'll have a talk with her tomorrow."

Sage looked at Emily. "Ghosts travel faster than people, you know."

"I figured."

"Mrs. Thompson knew about the murder before you did, because Helen Harper's ghost suddenly shot into the house and started screaming that someone had killed her."

Sage told Emily that communicating with Mrs. Thompson wasn't much different than having a conversation with Emily: it was easy enough that she didn't feel worn out afterward. Talking to a brand-new ghost and establishing a rapport with them, on the other hand, would be a lot of effort. Sage promised to return the next night for a proper séance with Helen Harper.

"I've got clients at Seeing Beyond until three, then I'll go home and rest up before coming here," Sage assured Emily. "Mrs. Thompson did channel some information from Helen, though. More of an image, really. Helen was grabbed from behind, and a hand clamped over her mouth."

Emily sighed sadly. "She couldn't call for help, even though she wasn't that far away from the other witches."

"She struggled briefly, and then she felt a knife go into her chest," Sage continued. "Mrs. Thompson gave me the impression that Helen didn't see her attacker, unfortunately."

"Then tomorrow we'll ask Helen who would have had a good reason to stab her to death." Emily shivered. "Somebody walked out of this house with a knife, knowing they were going to kill Helen with it. And now, we're all staying together."

"I don't think you're in danger, but all the same, lock your bedroom door. And hope Darlene isn't the killer!"

"Thanks for the comforting words," Emily said sarcastically, but the last part was broken by a wide yawn. She glanced at her watch and saw it was just after midnight. "Let's both get to bed. I have a feeling tomorrow is going to be a long day."

Darlene was already asleep by the time Emily saw Sage off, locked the front door, and returned to her bedroom. Between being tired and not wanting to disturb Darlene, Emily simply slipped off her shoes and crawled carefully into bed. Her last thought before drifting off was a wish for the murderer to be anyone but her mother-in-law.

When Emily's alarm went off at six o'clock Friday morning, Emily quickly silenced it, then glanced at the other side of the bed. The noise hadn't woken Darlene, so Emily got up and moved as quietly as she could. Soon, she was dressed and in the kitchen, staring at the coffee maker while willing it to brew faster.

Emily had enough sliced meats and cheeses for all of her guests, but she would be in short supply of Grainy Day baked goods, since she now had six guests instead of four. With a shrug, she arranged what she had onto trays and carried them to the dining room. It was already after seven, the usual time she put out breakfast, but she hadn't heard so much as a footstep from upstairs yet.

Emily was just finishing arranging the trays on the sideboard when she thought she heard a quiet knock.

"Mrs. Thompson?" Emily called in a half-whisper.

After a few moments, Emily heard the quiet sound again, but this time, it was clear the knocking was coming from the front door. She opened it and saw Trevor Williams standing there, his dark hair disheveled and his blue eyes worried. "Hey, you okay?" he asked quietly. "I heard the news."

Emily sighed. After a lifetime in Oak Hill, it should have been no surprise how fast gossip traveled, but the speed with which news of Helen's murder had spread was astonishing. Emily made a mental note to be prepared for a phone call from her mother soon, wanting to know every detail. "I'm okay," Emily said. "My guests are still asleep, so we can sit out here on the swing. You want some coffee?"

"Yes, please." Trevor followed Emily down the hall to the kitchen and put a white box on the countertop before pouring himself a cup of coffee.

"Did you bring biscuits?" Emily hadn't noticed the familiar white box before, but now she eyed it hungrily.

"Yeah, I heard you wound up with a whole group under house arrest, so I figured you might be short for breakfast. I picked up a dozen of Trish's murder biscuits before coming over."

Emily put an arm around Trevor and gave him a side-ways hug, careful not to upset his steaming coffee. "You're a lifesaver! Thank you, Trevor!" Emily opened the box and took four biscuits out, then put them on a small plate. The remaining eight would be more than enough for the two extra mouths she had to feed.

Trevor offered to carry the plate while Emily refilled her own coffee cup, then took the carafe to the dining room. Whenever her guests were finally up and moving, their breakfast and coffee would be waiting for them.

Once Trevor and Emily were settled onto the swing on the front porch, Emily took a giant bite of a biscuit. As she chewed, she eyed the two police officers, who had set up a small pop-up canopy in the front yard and were now sitting in chairs beneath it, facing the house. Emily gave them a hesitant little wave.

After she finally swallowed, she said, "Sorry. Last night

was long and difficult, and I didn't realize how hungry it had made me."

"I heard it was one of your guests who died, and probably one of your guests who killed them," Trevor prompted.

"I only had four guests, and one of them was Helen, the one who was stabbed. There were another three ladies staying downtown, but the police wanted to corral everyone here until they figure out who's guilty."

Trevor picked at his biscuit, little white flakes floating down toward his feet. "I don't like the idea of you staying in the same house as a murderer."

"I don't like it, either, but I'm a prisoner in my own house until this is sorted out."

"Surely you can still come and go," Trevor said in surprise. "I doubt you're a suspect."

"Good point. I'll ask Danny if I'm allowed to wander off. Honestly, though, I don't think I'll leave the house much, if at all. I don't want my guests to feel like I'm abandoning them. I still need to clean rooms, answer the phone, and make sure everyone is fed. Speaking of which, I wonder if the police will be throwing us a pizza party for dinner? I don't have enough food on hand to cook for everyone."

"If you're not willing to leave, then do you want me to stay? I feel like it's just you versus a whole coven of witches, and I'm not sure I like that."

"One," Emily said, holding up a finger, "do you even believe in witches?" She raised a second finger. "Two, one of them is Scott's mom, so I don't feel like I'm all that alone in this."

Trevor frowned. "Don't *you* believe in witches? I would have expected you to, especially if your mother-in-law is one."

"I didn't know she was until this week. Sage explained

51

that witchcraft is really about manipulating energy, which I guess makes sense, but I'm still on the skeptic's side of the fence."

"I've told you before that I visited a lot of psychics when I was trying to locate my brother," Trevor said, finally putting his uneaten biscuit back down onto the plate that sat on the swing between himself and Emily. "Sage is the first one I met whose abilities I actually believed in. But, even though I visited fraud after fraud, the idea of learning to use some sort of sixth sense has been around for thousands of years. For it to last so long, I figured there was some kernel of truth in it. The same goes with witches. If they really, truly couldn't do anything at all, the very idea of them would have faded into legends and historic footnotes already."

Emily took another bite as she pondered Trevor's words. Before learning Sage was a psychic medium, Emily had always been skeptical about anyone who claimed to communicate with the dead. As a child, she had always thought ghost stories were just that—stories—before her grandparents began reporting unusual activity in the Victorian home they had bought and turned into Eternal Rest.

"Okay," Emily finally said, nodding her head. "I'm going to try to be more open-minded about witches, especially when it comes to this particular coven. If they really have a killer in their midst, they might need a little magic to sort it all out."

Trevor finally began to eat as the conversation drifted toward speculating what sorts of things witches could actually do. By then, Emily could hear the occasional voice from inside, and she knew her guests were awake. "I should get back in there," she said reluctantly.

When Trevor offered again to stay, telling Emily he had actually taken the day off work to come check on her,

Emily suggested an alternative. "You can help me set up some fans out there in the tent. It's going to be hot again today. Then, if you're up for it, I've got a few errands that need to be run. I'll give you my credit card and a list."

Trevor readily agreed. He and Emily got two large floor fans out of the basement along with some extension cords, and soon, the tent had a nice breeze flowing through it. Just as Trevor pulled out of the driveway, armed with a shopping list, Emily saw Danny's truck pulling in, with two patrol cars and a van right behind it. Emily had followed Trevor onto the front porch to give him last-minute instructions about how thick the deli meat should be sliced, so she simply waited on the top step for the new arrivals.

"How are you this morning?" Danny asked as he walked up.

"Tired, but otherwise okay," Emily answered.

"And your guests?"

"I don't actually know. I've been out here since before they got up. I assume you're here to talk with all of them again?"

Danny nodded grimly. "Yes, I'll be digging into their relationships with Helen. The officers who guarded the house all night are being relieved by their replacements, and the forensics team is going to take a look at Helen's room."

"Wow, my house is going to be crowded. Come on in. I've got coffee, but not enough breakfast to go around."

"That's okay," said an officer who was stepping up next to Danny. "We brought biscuits and croissants from Grainy Day."

Emily actually laughed. Trish was making a good profit off Helen's murder.

Danny questioned each witch one at a time while Emily cleaned rooms, caught up on emails, and did other tasks around the house. When Danny was done, he found

Emily in the kitchen and called her into the parlor. The six women were already seated there—Serenity was sitting cross-legged on the floor, while the others occupied the sofa and wingback chairs. Emily pulled her desk chair over to the group and sat down, looking at Danny expectantly.

"Ladies," Danny said, addressing the witches, "every single one of you refused to say exactly what you were doing in the cemetery. However, a couple of you mentioned you were spread out along 'the circle.' Initially, I thought you meant the circular wall of the cemetery. Then, I began to realize your circle is something entirely different. You need to tell Emily why you're here."

Abbie looked at Emily with a judgmental frown. "She's not part of the coven, and neither are you. Our business here is our own."

"Your business here affects Emily more than you can imagine," Danny countered.

"She deserves to know," Darlene said, giving Abbie a challenging stare. "We're on her land, and I don't want her to think we're up to anything bad out here."

Abbie pursed her lips. "And the rest of you? Do you agree Emily should know?"

"She's worthy," Serenity said airily.

"She is," Malena agreed, "but is the detective?"

Danny crossed his arms over his chest, looking like a dad lecturing a roomful of wayward daughters. "It doesn't matter whether I am or not, because I already figured it out. I'll tell Emily myself if I have to, but it would mean more coming from all of you."

"Darlene, you tell her," Evelyne said encouragingly.

Darlene got off the sofa and walked over to Emily. She took Emily's hand as she looked down at her and said, "Emily, honey, you have ghosts here, but have you ever noticed there aren't really evil entities in Oak Hill? No demons, no malicious ghosts, and no stories of hauntings like you see in horror movies."

Emily gasped. "This is about the psychic barrier!"

Darlene was so surprised she dropped Emily's hand and stepped back. "You already know about it?"

Emily just nodded.

Several of the witches began whispering to each other, but Darlene continued, "The energy of the barrier wanes over time, so every ten years, we gather to renew it. We raise energy three nights in a row, then on the fourth night —the night of a full moon, always—we send all of that energy to the barrier to make it strong again. After Sunday, that barrier will be as solid as it was the day we put it there."

Emily jumped up from her chair. "No! You can't! If you strengthen the barrier, Scott will be trapped outside it for another ten years! We're so close to getting him home!"

Darlene blinked at Emily. She pressed a hand against her chest, and her eyes filled with tears. "Scott? You mean my Scott?"

8

Emily pressed her hands to her mouth as she felt her face crumple. Tears began to slide down her cheeks, and she said through her fingers, "Darlene, I'm so sorry. I should have told you. I didn't mean for you to find out like this. It just came out before I could stop myself."

"I don't understand." Darlene sniffed loudly, and she pulled a tissue out of her pocket and began to dab at her nose. "Why is Scott's ghost still here? He should have crossed over. And why would he be stuck outside the barrier? It's made to keep evil things at bay, not good souls like his."

"We—Sage and I—think Scott's crash on the way home from visiting you almost three years ago wasn't just an accident. I never believed it was. His car veered off a straight stretch of road in the middle of nowhere. There were no other cars to avoid, no mechanical problems with the car, he wasn't texting... Plus, right before he left your house to come back home, he called and told me we needed to find ways to protect Eternal Rest spiritually."

Darlene groped toward Emily and grabbed her arm. "I need to sit down," she said quietly, her voice wavering.

Emily guided her gently into the desk chair, keeping a comforting hand on Darlene's shoulder. "One of my ghosts here sensed Scott's presence," Emily continued. "He was weak, and we learned there was a psychic barrier around Oak Hill, and it runs just beyond the cemetery. Scott can't get through, so I sent my ghosts to look for him. He's being held captive by some kind of dark entity, and that entity is draining Scott's energy, making him too weak to cross through the barrier."

Darlene turned her head and pressed her cheek against Emily's forearm. "I should have known. There was a little part of me that also thought his crash was no accident, but I didn't want to accept it. The first night of his visit, he was fine. The next night, Scott said he had a nightmare about being chased by a shadowy black form. On the third night, the nightmare returned, and it was so bad I could hear him shouting in his sleep." Darlene looked at Emily, tears again forming in her eyes. "I don't think it was just a nightmare. And I think whatever was haunting him followed him when he left and made him crash."

Emily sank down until she was kneeling on the floor, her forehead resting on Darlene's leg. All she could do was cry. She couldn't imagine why a dark entity had targeted Scott, or how scared he must have been if he had felt the need to protect their house.

After so long, she finally knew for certain Scott's crash had been caused by some kind of paranormal entity. Instead of feeling relieved to have her suspicions confirmed, Emily only felt a renewed grief. What had happened on that drive? Had Scott fought with the entity? Had he known he was going to die before the car swerved off the road?

Darlene stroked Emily's hair, trying to give her daughter-in-law some comfort, even though Emily could hear her crying, too.

As her tears began to slow, Emily suddenly became

conscious that everyone was staring at her. She couldn't see anyone, but she could feel the attention like a physical force. She raised her head and wiped at her cheeks. "I'm going to take a walk," she announced.

Darlene seemed to understand Emily needed to be alone, and she simply nodded knowingly. Emily was out the front door and halfway down the steps before she realized she had been followed.

"Emily, stop," Danny called.

Emily glanced over her shoulder but kept walking.

"Emily! Wait!"

Turning, Emily saw Danny's look of sympathy. It just made her feel worse.

"I'm sorry," he said. "A few of them talked about a circle, and how they were raising energy, and I just knew they meant the barrier. You needed to know."

"I did." Emily nodded. "I'm just upset to know I was right about Scott's crash."

Danny stepped forward and curled a hand gently around her shoulder. "I'll help you find and get rid of this entity as best I can. I'm not psychic, but I'll support you."

Emily nodded. "I know you will. Thank you." She stepped back. "I'm going to the cemetery. I need some time to myself."

Danny looked like he was going to argue against that, but Emily didn't wait for him to respond. She turned and walked quickly toward the front gate of Hilltop Cemetery. One of the police officers on guard duty called out to her, but Emily heard Danny behind her saying, "It's okay. She's not one of the suspects."

Instead of walking to the top of the hill, Emily turned right onto the lowest path that ringed the hill. She continued her fast pace until Eternal Rest was out of sight behind her. She didn't want to be seen by anyone as she fought to control her feelings.

Finally, Emily stepped off the brick path and made her way to a rickety wrought-iron bench that sat at the foot of a large oak tree. The bench faced a row of three headstones, all with a different style of cross on top. Emily sank onto the bench and leaned forward to rest her forehead on her clasped hands, her elbows propped on her knees. She inhaled slowly while focusing on the sound of the oak leaves stirring above her and the chatter of nearby birds.

*Why didn't he tell me about the nightmares? Scott must have suspected they were more than just dreams, or he wouldn't have said we needed to put up spiritual protections around Eternal Rest. Did he know what was chasing after him? Had he expected it to follow him home?*

Lost in thoughts like those, Emily didn't even know someone had walked up to her until she heard her name being called. She looked up and saw dark-brown eyes staring back at her. Usually, Reed Marshall's eyes had a mischievous look, but at the moment, they were full of concern.

Reed sat down next to Emily. "Are you upset about the murder here?"

"Yes, but I'm more upset about Scott." Emily poured out every detail of what Darlene had said and how the witches were the ones who had put the psychic barrier in place. She had told Danny she wanted to be alone, but it turned out she simply wanted to be with the right friend.

Reed put a comforting arm around Emily's shoulders as he listened. When she was finally done, he said, "I know it's upsetting news, but this could be beneficial information. It might help us learn more about what's keeping Scott bound and how to help him."

"You're right," Emily conceded. She looked at Reed apologetically. "Sorry you've got another crime scene here."

"Bodies need to stop showing up in my cemeteries,"

Reed answered disdainfully. "None of the other sextons I know have had this problem. I've had one murder victim at The Garden, and that's two now here at Hilltop. And this victim was the leader of a coven of witches, right?"

"Right. Helen Harper. I get the impression from the others that Helen wasn't all that well-liked. One of them, Abbie, seems to be her only friend in the coven, but even the two of them were having a disagreement about something the day they arrived."

"I was just over there talking to the police." Reed jerked his chin toward the southwest corner of the cemetery. "They still haven't found the murder weapon, so there's a chance one of your guests brought it back to the house with them."

"That's creepy."

"Expect Eternal Rest to get turned upside down later. The police will probably do a search."

After Helen's murder and the news about both the barrier and Scott, Emily didn't have the energy to really care whether the police wanted to search her house. She shrugged. "Maybe they'll find that blue sock of mine that went missing while they're at it."

Reed stayed with Emily for a while, but once she was calmer, Reed said he needed to get back to work. He gave Emily a tight hug before heading up the hill to the plot he and his team were working on that day.

Emily felt like she was almost ready to face her guests again, and she was about to rise when she saw Malena walking up the path. Malena spotted Emily and made a beeline for her. Instead of sitting on the bench, Malena leaned against an iron fence that surrounded a nearby plot.

"One of the police officers is following me to make sure I don't take off," she said, sounding torn between amusement and annoyance. "I guess we're allowed to walk around the house and the cemetery, but we can't be out of sight."

"I'm really sorry about all this," Emily said.

*Why am I apologizing? I didn't kill anyone or force an entire coven to be stuck in my home.*

"You're upset that we came here to renew the barrier, because right now, it's weak enough that your late husband's spirit actually has a chance to get through. You're afraid he'll have to wait until the cycle wanes again." Malena wasn't asking a question, and Emily admired the way she summed up the situation so succinctly.

When Emily just nodded once, Malena continued, "We all try our best to keep our loved ones safe, but we can't plan for every possibility. Your husband was outside the barrier, so it couldn't protect him, but by keeping it strong, it will save others in this town. There are thousands of people living here who have no idea that we're watching over them and keeping them safe."

"And a lot of ghosts, too," Emily said. She thought of all the ghosts Kelly and Sage had either seen or sensed coming through the barrier and heading toward downtown Oak Hill. "I think ghosts know about the barrier, and they're spreading the word. They've been flocking here in recent weeks."

Malena gazed toward the western edge of the cemetery. "Really? I wonder how they found out."

"I don't know, but my guess is they're coming through now, while the barrier is weak, so that when it's strong again, they'll be protected from dark things, too."

"I'm glad we can help the living and the dead, especially when we can't seem to help ourselves." Malena sighed. "We don't have a good track record when it comes to our coven leaders. First Evelyne got ousted in a ridiculously silly scandal, and now Helen is dead."

"Evelyne used to be coven leader?"

"Oh, yes. She's hated Helen ever since for taking the position that she felt should be hers until she died."

"Except Helen is the one who had the position until she died."

"Exactly."

9

Emily and Malena walked back to the house together. Malena wouldn't give up any details about the scandal she had alluded to, saying she hadn't been involved in the situation and that she considered Evelyne a friend. "Evelyne herself won't really talk about it, so the details I have came from Helen," Malena said. "I'm pretty sure her telling was embellished a bit."

Malena's refusal to give details meant the two women moved on to discussing more mundane subjects during the walk, like how humid it was and what to do about lunch. Emily actually perked up when Malena said Danny had put in a lunch order with The Depot, and that "the nice officer with the hair that's gray at the temples" would be delivering it. Emily was grateful to know both food and Roger were on the way.

Even though Emily still felt some trepidation about going back into a crowded house with no idea who among them had killed Helen, she at least knew she could bury herself in work while waiting for lunch to arrive. The outside world didn't know what was going on at Eternal Rest, and the reservation requests were still pouring in.

Danny came to check on Emily, but she simply told him she was feeling better and that the walk had done her good. She was relieved when he announced the police were done with the search of Helen's room, and that she could put one of her guests in it. "And that means I'm heading out," Danny concluded. "I know I'll have follow-up questions, but I've got a lot of information and statements to pore through, so I expect I'll be glued to my desk at the station until late tonight. We'll need to search the other guest rooms to look for our murder weapon, but I want to sift through everything that we learned today first. It could help us know whose room to start with."

"I'll walk you out," Emily said, rising. "Thanks for your help. And thanks for ordering lunch for everyone! It saves me a lot of trouble."

Emily walked down the porch steps with Danny, then said quietly, "Do you have any idea yet who might have killed Helen?"

Danny shook his head. "Every single one of those women had some kind of a grudge against Helen, and none of them are saying as much as they know."

At the sound of a car turning into the driveway, Emily looked up expectantly, assuming lunch had arrived. Instead, it was Trevor, back from running his errands.

Danny urged Emily to be on guard and to pass on anything she and Sage might learn from Helen's ghost. As he spoke, Trevor parked, got out of his car, and began to carry shopping bags toward the house.

Trevor stopped at the foot of the stairs and looked hard at Emily. "Something bad happened."

"Something bad happened almost three years ago, just as I had suspected."

Trevor's expression was grim. "Scott's death actually was tied to that entity, then. You've confirmed it."

Emily just nodded and bit her lip, willing herself not to get upset again.

"Take care, Emily," Danny said. "I'll keep you posted on anything I learn."

"Thanks, Danny." Emily noticed he wasn't looking at her. Rather, he seemed to be eyeing Trevor. Danny nodded at him as he passed, but his face was stoic.

Emily met Trevor at the bottom of the stairs and reached out for some of the shopping bags. "I'll help you with these, and then I'll fill you in."

Emily gave Trevor a brief account of Darlene's news while putting away the groceries. Somehow, it was less upsetting to tell the story because she was doing something else at the same time. The little distraction of putting away milk and butter kept her from crying again.

Emily plunked a loaf of bread onto the counter as she ended with, "So, now, the witches want to strengthen the barrier, and I know it's important, but at what cost? Scott will be trapped outside it unless he somehow gets through before Sunday night."

Trevor didn't have an answer for that, but he gently spun Emily toward him and wrapped his arms around her in a fierce hug. After a moment, Emily pulled away and sniffed. "I'm going to start crying again if I'm not careful."

"Then cry. Sometimes it's exactly what you need."

Emily wondered how much Trevor had cried since his dad had died just a couple of weeks before. Wanting to lighten the mood, she said, "What I need right now is lunch. I'm starving."

The doorbell rang at that moment, and Emily knew it would be Roger with the food. Soon, Styrofoam containers full of sandwiches, potato chips, and chocolate chip cookies were arrayed on the dining room table, and everyone was eagerly digging in.

The witches decided to take their lunch out to the tent, and Roger said he was going to head to the crime scene in the cemetery to see what was going on there, which left Emily and Trevor with Eternal Rest to themselves.

"Thanks for running errands for me," Emily said

between big bites of a club sandwich. Jay, the owner of The Depot, had sent over a variety of sandwiches, but he had written Emily's name on the wrapper for the club sandwich, knowing it was her favorite. "If you hadn't done all of that for me, I wouldn't have been here to learn about Scott's nightmares or the barrier."

"I'm happy to help. I can't talk to ghosts for you, but I'm pretty skilled with a shopping cart."

Sage arrived just as Trevor and Emily were wrapping up lunch. She didn't even bother to knock, and she swept into the dining room with a look of concern. "Tell me everything I've missed, right now," she demanded. "There's a weird vibe in this house. Tension and a sense of urgency. It's different than what I felt here last night. Don't skip a single detail."

With that, Sage sat down and pulled an egg salad sandwich toward her. She ate while Emily talked, even though she was getting tired of repeating that morning's revelations. When she talked about the psychic barrier, Sage nodded her head, swallowed, and said, "Of course! That makes so much sense! I had thought maybe psychic mediums had put it there, but witches would be able to channel that kind of energy, too."

"We have to stop them, Sage," Emily said earnestly. "I can't take it if Scott is trapped outside the barrier for another ten years."

Sage looked slightly surprised. "That barrier is important, Em. Remember, that dark entity lunged at you a couple days ago. You want that thing to come through and terrorize you in your own home?"

"Of course not."

"Obviously, we just have to get Scott through the barrier by the end of the weekend."

"Oh, no problem," Emily scoffed. "And solve a murder while we're at it."

"Easy peasy." Sage grinned. Even as tired as she was from all the ghosts draining her energy, she still couldn't resist a challenge.

Sage's positivity made Emily feel better about what they were up against, and she felt more peaceful than she had since the morning's revelations.

Sage was still chewing the last bite of her cookie as she began to pull her séance tools out of the bag she had brought with her. "I'm glad your guests are outside. I don't want any of them to suspect they might be a suspect! It's time to find out what kind of gossip Helen Harper can give us about her coven. Almost time, that is."

Sage finished setting up her purple seven-day candle, bell, pencil, paper, and silver dollar, then sat back with her hands folded. When there was a knock on the door, Sage rose dramatically. "Now it's time!"

She told Emily to stay put while she answered the door, and soon, Sage returned to the dining room with Reed in tow. "I called Reed in to add his perceptiveness and energy to our session," Sage explained. "Plus, he's just good moral support. Let's get started!"

Reed shut the door and turned off the dining room lights while Emily got up and closed the curtains. It was a bright, sunny afternoon, and the relative dimness of the dining room felt comforting, like a little oasis from the heat outside.

Sage lit the candle, then took a deep breath and closed her eyes. She began to address the ghost of Helen in a flat, almost monotone voice. "Helen Harper, we met yesterday, and I promised I would be back to help you. I don't have a lot of energy these days, so the faster you can share information with us, the better. We know you were murdered by someone in your coven. We also know you didn't see your killer. Can you tell us which woman in your coven might have wanted to kill you?"

Sage was quiet for a long moment. "Helen is sending me wave after wave of emotion, but she's not pointing out anyone specific. I sense that she was fearful, like—" Sage broke off and furrowed her brow in concentration. "Oh, I see. That's valuable information, Helen."

Sage opened her eyes and peered around the table at Emily, Trevor, and Reed. "Helen felt that her position as coven leader put her in a dangerous spot. She believed it made her a target. I don't know how she became coven leader, but I don't think she won the position by popular vote."

"Evelyne was the coven leader before Helen," Emily noted. "Apparently, it was some kind of scandal that got her replaced, and Helen was somehow involved in bringing it to light. Can you ask her about that?"

Sage closed her eyes again and asked, "Helen, what happened between you and Evelyne?"

Sage's head moved slowly back and forth. "I'm seeing candles, a little doll, and a needle and thread. Evelyne is working a spell against Helen. A spell for what, Helen?"

After another prolonged silence, Sage suddenly laughed loudly. "A spell to shut you up? What were you saying about Evelyne that made her feel the need to do that?"

A quiet but constant noise made Emily look down at the table, and she saw the silver dollar sliding slowly toward Sage. "Was Helen saying something about money?" she asked Sage.

Suddenly, the coin tipped up on its edge and fell over on its other side.

"I don't understand," Sage said. She leaned forward, her eyes squeezed tightly shut. "Flipped? Flipped over? Oh, I see! Evelyne would say one thing, then do the opposite."

A few moments later, Sage opened her eyes again and

spoke in her normal voice. "It seems Evelyne was lying to her coven, and Helen called her out on it. Helen showed me Evelyne promising to work an abundance spell on their behalf, then working a bad luck spell instead. Apparently, this started happening a lot, and she was finally replaced by Helen as coven leader."

"Why would Evelyne do that to her coven?" It made no sense to Emily.

Sage closed her eyes again and asked Helen that exact question. The silence lasted for at least five minutes, punctuated now and then by Sage clicking her tongue or making quiet noises of disapproval. Eventually, Sage said, "Thank you, Helen. This has been very helpful."

"What did she say?" Reed asked.

"Helen believes Evelyne was simply on a power trip. The more her coven needed her, the better she felt. She cast spells to make life harder for the witches so they would come to her for help. Ugh. How manipulative."

"That's the story according to Helen," Emily pointed out. She picked up the silver dollar. "There are two sides to every coin."

"Agreed. According to Helen, Evelyne had good motive to kill her: she lost her position and her power because of Helen. I think our next chat needs to be with Evelyne. You'll have to do that, Em. I'm nearly spent already."

Emily was already standing up to open the curtains and turn on the lights when Sage suddenly stiffened. Her hands gripped the edge of the table, and her eyes stared straight ahead, as if transfixed. Sage's mouth opened, but Emily couldn't tell if she was trying to cry out or if it was an expression of surprise.

Reed stood. "Helen Harper, you stop whatever you're doing, right now." His voice was firm and confident.

"Remember, Sage is here to help you, and you would be wise to treat her with respect."

Sage's body relaxed abruptly, and she shook her head quickly. "Oh, what a horrible woman!"

"Did Helen show you something else that Evelyne did to her?" Emily asked.

"No, I'm talking about Helen! She nearly possessed me just now. I held her off, but just barely. She wanted to show me the magic she worked against Evelyne in retaliation for what she did to the coven."

"What kind of magic?"

"It looked like dark magic," Sage said, her voice trembling. "I saw Helen drawing faces with Xs for eyes. She was burning some kind of herbs and chanting. I think Helen wanted to kill Evelyne."

Sage left Eternal Rest shortly after wrapping up the séance, saying she needed a nap. Emily offered up Helen's vacant room, but Sage declined, worried Helen would try to invade her mind again the second she fell asleep and let her psychic guard down.

"But," Sage said, holding up a commanding finger as she stood at the front door, "I want you to tell me everything you learn from Evelyne."

"First I'm going to call Danny and tell him any interesting tidbits. You'll be second on my list."

Reed had to get back to the cemetery to wrap up work for the day. As he followed Sage onto the front porch, he turned back to Emily and said, "Don't you miss guests who were just ordinary tourists?" He winked and started on his way toward Hilltop before Emily could think of a good answer.

Emily glanced at Trevor, her eyebrows raised. He crossed his arms and leaned against the dining room doorway. "I'm not leaving. Not yet."

"Good." Emily shut the front door and led the way into the parlor. "I want to talk to Evelyne, alone. I need to get her away from the coven, and I think you might be able to help me do it."

Trevor grinned. "Are we hatching a plan to catch a murderer?"

"It's not quite that dramatic. I just want to ask her a few questions, like whether she was really working spells to give her own coven bad luck."

"Fine, then." Trevor made a face of mock disappointment. "I suppose we can't just walk up to her and ask if she killed Helen before Helen could kill her."

"No, we can't. Instead, I think you should ask her something very different. Once they're back in here, I want you to approach Evelyne and tell her you're looking for a little magical help."

"What kind of help?"

Emily spread her hands. "Any kind! Career, money, love—take your pick. If you ask nicely, I bet she'll take you aside to give you some witchy wisdom."

"And then I hand her off to you for questioning."

"See if you can get her to come to the kitchen. We can talk in there."

Not only did Trevor agree, but he looked excited at his undercover role. When the witches returned to the house a short while later, Emily was again at her desk while Trevor sat on the sofa, talking on his cell phone to one of his clients from the graphic design firm he worked for.

Some of the witches headed up the stairs, but Evelyne and Serenity came into the parlor. As they entered, Trevor turned to Emily and surreptitiously gave her a thumbs up before wrapping up his call.

Instead of sticking with Emily's plan, though, Trevor turned to Serenity and said, "You look like the type of witch who knows about..." The rest of Trevor's words were too quiet for Emily to hear as he leaned toward Serenity and whispered in her ear.

Serenity pulled back and gave Trevor a knowing look.

"Oh, of course. But there are important guidelines to follow. Would you like a quick lesson?"

"Yes, please, if you don't mind."

"Not at all! Let's go sit in the tent, where we'll have some privacy." The small smile on Serenity's lips made her look even more like a fairy.

Trevor might have made up his own plan, but Emily had to hand it to him as he walked out the front door with Serenity: he had found a way to get Emily and Evelyne alone in the same room.

Knowing one of the other witches might come into the parlor at any moment, Emily wasted no time in hurrying over to the sofa. She sat down next to Evelyne and put on her best sympathetic expression. "Sage held a séance here while you were all outside. Helen channeled images through Sage. She really made your life as coven leader hard, didn't she?"

Evelyne's face took on a guarded look. "Are you asking me if I had a reason to kill Helen?"

*Yes, I am.* Emily thought the words, but of course she couldn't say them out loud. Instead, she said smoothly, "What I want to know is whether Helen was working dark magic against you or anyone else in the coven. Helen really scared Sage with some of the things she channeled through her."

"Dark magic? Not that I know of, but I certainly wouldn't put it past her." Evelyne's expression relaxed, and she sat back against the sofa. "Helen actually accused *me* of working dark magic. She told everyone in the coven I was trying to make their lives miserable. Why would I do that? I wanted the girls to be prosperous under my leadership. I wanted them to have such fulfilling lives that they would thank me for helping them work the proper magic to make all their dreams come true."

So Helen had been right, at least, in sensing that

Evelyne had been on a power trip. Whichever version of the story was correct—or if the truth was something in between, as Emily expected—it was clear Evelyne liked being at the top of the witch hierarchy. She wanted to be needed. And, if Helen really had been working a death spell against Evelyne, then Evelyne didn't seem to realize it. Evelyne certainly had good reason to dislike Helen for getting her ousted as coven leader, and she was still a suspect in Emily's eyes, but she certainly hadn't killed Helen in self-defense against a death spell.

As the afternoon wore away, Emily suddenly realized she had the downstairs to herself. The witches had gone upstairs. Emily had put fresh sheets on the bed that had been Helen's, and she had swapped out the bath towels for clean ones, so Darlene had moved into that room. Emily assumed her guests were napping after a long morning of being questioned by Danny.

Only one of the witches wasn't resting. Serenity and Trevor were still outside, and Emily wondered what kind of magic Trevor wanted to learn that was taking such a long time.

When the two of them did finally return to the house, it was late enough that Trevor was carrying goods from Grainy Day. "Trish swung by with these," he told Emily as he paused in the parlor doorway. "I was just coming back into the house, so I said I'd bring them in. She agreed, but she also made me promise to tell you to call her so you can catch her up on the latest."

Emily laughed as Trevor continued on to the kitchen. Of course Trish would want to know the latest gossip from Eternal Rest.

At seven, the doorbell rang, and Emily answered it to find herself face-to-face with a stack of pizza boxes. A teenager's wide-eyed face leaned around the side of the stack, and he said, "I have a delivery for a Darlene?" His eyes kept darting past Emily.

"I'll take them for her," Emily offered, reaching out. "What do I owe you?"

"She paid over the phone when she ordered." The teen wasn't even pretending to look at Emily anymore, and he actually craned his neck in an effort to peer into the parlor. "She included a nice tip, so I should thank her. You sure she doesn't want to come get them herself? Or maybe one of your other guests?"

Emily glanced down at her dark-blue button-down shirt, which had *Eternal Rest Bed and Breakfast* embroidered in silver on the left breast. Clearly, Emily was not only the owner of Eternal Rest, but also not a suspect. She assumed that was the reason the teenager wanted to get a glimpse of one of her guests. He wanted to see someone who might be a murderer.

"You can read about it in the newspaper, or just go to The Depot and ask the owner there to fill you in," Emily said patiently, telling herself not to laugh at the absurd situation.

The teen's shoulders sagged after he handed Emily the pizzas. "Okay. Night." He turned and walked back to his car, throwing glances over his shoulder toward the upstairs windows as he went.

There were five pizzas in all, and Emily was surprised that her six guests felt the need for so much food. When she knocked on the door to Darlene's room and told her dinner had arrived, Darlene explained they had ordered extra so they could just eat the leftovers for lunch the next day. "Plus," Darlene said, looking embarrassed, "we had a hard time agreeing on what toppings to get. On the upside, there's enough here for you, too!"

Emily stacked plates and napkins on the dining room table, next to the pizzas, while Darlene let the other women know dinner was being served. As Piper came into the room, she was just turning to speak to Malena. "Of course, I need to carry some extra charms with me tonight. I just feel like I need the boost for our ritual."

Emily had piled pizza slices onto plates for herself and Trevor, planning to return to the parlor, but she stopped at Piper's words. "You're planning to move forward with the rituals, then?"

"Of course." Serenity had just walked in, catching Emily's question. "Why wouldn't we?"

"Because Scott is still stuck outside the barrier." Emily wanted to shout the words at the women. Why couldn't they understand how desperate she was to bring the spirit of her husband home?

Serenity put a soft hand on Emily's arm, her pixie face looking almost comically sympathetic, with wide eyes below drawn-together eyebrows. "We know it's hard, Emily, but this is for the good of everyone in Oak Hill."

"It's like we discussed earlier, in the cemetery," Malena said. "We all want to protect our loved ones, and that's what this barrier is all about."

"But my loved one is stuck outside it, and I can't protect him!" Emily argued.

"I don't like it any more than you do," Darlene said. She was standing in the hallway just outside the dining room door. "Emily, I hate that we're interrupting your work to bring Scott across, but we will help you find him beyond the barrier. We will work to give him peace. I promise you that."

"We will," Serenity said. "We aren't asking you to abandon him, and we aren't going to abandon him, either, now that we know. We just have to find a different way."

Emily took a deep breath. "Okay," she finally said. With three of the women all telling her the same thing, that meant at least half the coven wanted to move forward with restoring the barrier. There didn't seem any point in trying to convince them otherwise.

When Emily reached the parlor and handed Trevor his plate, she said, "Want to see witches at work later? They're going back to the cemetery for the second night of an energy-raising ritual. This time, I'm going with them to make sure no one else gets killed in my cemetery."

"I'm not going to lie, Emily. I'm fascinated by all of this, especially after talking to Serenity this afternoon. I'd love to come along."

Trevor had a definite bounce in his step as he and Emily walked toward Hilltop an hour later. The group heading to the cemetery was a strange one. The six witches led the way, followed by two of the police officers who had been on guard duty outside the house. They had insisted on coming, saying they needed to keep everyone in their line of sight. Emily and Trevor trailed after them, though the group had to wait on Emily to unlock the iron gate before they could continue up the hill.

When the witches reached the top of the hill, they went a short distance down the far side, where Abbie called them to a halt. "Spread out, like we did last night," Abbie instructed. "Evelyne, you go to the north end. I'll take the south so I can begin the chant."

As the women began to spread out, one of the police officers warned them not to put too much distance between themselves. "We need all of you in sight at all times," he reminded them firmly.

Emily and Trevor stood a short distance behind Serenity and Darlene, who were in the middle of the line of witches. The police officers were flanking the line of women, both of them with crossed arms and stern, judgmental looks on their faces. Emily assumed they were skeptics about anything supernatural, just like Roger.

Darlene began to raise her arms upward, and Emily

knew the ritual was about to start. Impulsively, she dashed forward and put a hand on Darlene's shoulder. "Please," Emily begged. "Can't we help Scott first?"

"This has to be done, Emily." Darlene's voice was low, and over it, Emily could hear Abbie chanting, the power and confidence in her voice clear. "I meant it when I said we would help you. He's my son, and I'll do whatever it takes."

"Then stop this ritual. Let's help Scott before the barrier is strengthened."

Darlene looked forward again as Piper, who was next to Abbie, took up the chant. "This is how we keep Oak Hill safe," she whispered. "This is how we keep *you* safe."

Emily dropped her hand from Darlene's shoulder, but she remained standing behind her mother-in-law as Serenity repeated the chant. Soon, it was Darlene's turn, and she spoke clearly, calling on the elements to aid the witches in their work.

As Darlene spoke, Emily caught a faint shimmer in the night air. A glow above the trees at the bottom of the hill became brighter and brighter, until it formed the shape of a human. Green eyes shone like beacons toward the cemetery.

Darlene cut off in the middle of her chant, a choked cry escaping her lips. Her hands were still raised, palms outward, as she stared at the glowing figure. "Scott?" Her voice was filled with surprise and grief. "My dear boy, I see you!"

11

Emily put her arms around Darlene and held her as she cried. The shimmering form of Scott's ghost had faded into the night, but Darlene was still staring at the spot where he had appeared.

"That was him," Darlene said with a hiccup.

"Yes. That was Scott." Emily felt her own tears running down her cheeks.

"Oh, Darlene," Serenity said. Emily glanced to her left and realized the other witches had formed a circle around her and Darlene. Gentle hands reached out to touch Darlene's arms and shoulders in silent displays of comfort.

"We have to postpone the barrier renewal." Darlene's voice cracked. "We have to help my son first."

"No. I know he's your son, but he is only one man." Abbie spoke firmly but not unkindly. "There are thousands in this town. We have to protect them."

"But—" Darlene began.

"No."

Serenity and Malena both glanced briefly at Abbie, their brows furrowed, but neither woman spoke up.

"Darlene deserves to have her request carefully considered," Evelyne said, the challenge clear in her voice. "Helen is dead, which means we have no coven leader to guide us. We need to decide this together."

"And I assume you want your old job back?" Abbie said sharply.

Evelyne's eyes narrowed. "No. Even if I did, you'd beat me to it, I'm sure."

Piper made an impatient noise. "Stop it. We're not here tonight to decide who will be coven leader. Right now, we're doing a ritual to raise energy. Whether we decide to use that energy to strengthen the barrier or to help Darlene's son first, we still need to complete the ritual. Darlene, let's finish the ritual, and then we can discuss what happens next."

Darlene nodded. "You're right, Piper. Abbie, do you want to start over from the beginning?"

"I think that's best. Focus, ladies." Abbie moved away to retake her position along the line.

Emily gave Darlene a little squeeze, then let her go and stepped back. As the witches began to chant again, her chest tightened. Would Scott appear again as Darlene spoke? Had he showed up because he recognized the voice of his mother?

Darlene's turn was uneventful this time, and Emily wondered if Scott had expended all his energy the first time, or if the dark entity was keeping him from appearing again.

Emily was so focused on the sky above the treetops beyond Hilltop Cemetery that she didn't even notice when the ritual ended. She had been vaguely aware of chanting, some swaying, and the strong smell of burning incense, but she was so absorbed in looking for a sign of Scott that she really didn't register what the witches were doing. Suddenly, they were all standing in a group, facing Emily.

"Well?" Abbie prompted. "I said we're ready."

"Oh." Emily blinked. "Ready for what?"

"To go back to the house."

"Right. Of course." Emily looked at the sky one last

time. *Scott, if you can hear me, we saw you, and we're going to help you.* "Let's go."

Emily trudged toward Eternal Rest. Trevor walked silently at her side while the witches talked in excited tones about the ritual. Back at the house, Emily turned to go into the parlor, but Evelyne waved her into the dining room instead. "We have a lot to discuss," she began. "But first, we have some work to do. I want you to know what we're doing." Evelyne looked at Trevor and said sternly, "You need to wait in the parlor."

Trevor gave a nod. "Actually, I'm going to leave you ladies to it. Emily, I'll see you tomorrow. Call if you need anything."

"Thanks, Trevor," Emily said, already being ushered into the dining room by Serenity.

Darlene sat down wearily, and Malena scooted a chair close to her so she could speak quietly. Emily overheard the words "I understand" and "I know it's hard" as she murmured to Darlene.

Abbie stood at the head of the table while the other witches sat. Emily took up a spot near the dining room door, too anxious to sit. "Sisters," Abbie said loudly as the room fell silent, "we have two important tasks before us. Earlier, some of you were debating which to do first. I suggest we do both this weekend. If we can find a way to bring the spirit of Darlene's son through the barrier before Sunday night's strengthening ritual, then we can conclude this weekend knowing both he and the entire town of Oak Hill are safe."

Piper leaned forward. "How are we supposed to help this ghost in less than forty-eight hours? We don't even know where to start!"

Malena mumbled something unintelligible and stood. "I'll be right back." As she swept past Emily and headed upstairs, the remaining witches looked at each other in consternation, then turned almost as one to Abbie, the unasked question clear on all their faces: *How?*

Instead of looking at them, Abbie gazed calmly at Emily. "We're going to need your psychic friend."

"I'm sure she'll be happy to help," Emily answered. "However, as the barrier weakens, so does Sage. She may not be able to do much."

"Anything is better than nothing," Darlene said.

Malena's hurried footsteps sounded on the stairs, and soon, she came into the dining room with a thick book in her hands. The leather binding looked like it had originally been red, but time and wear had made it nearly black. Emily saw a flash of gold writing on the front, but even as she was trying to read the letters, Malena opened the book and set it on the table.

"Witchcraft goes back four generations in my family," she said, a clear note of pride in her voice. "I have a lot of knowledge from my foremothers in this grimoire, and I'm sure all of you have your own resources. We're looking for a way to strengthen a spirit."

"Or a way to punch a hole in the barrier," Piper pointed out.

"Exactly. Either we make Scott stronger, or we make the barrier weaker. Either one only needs to last long enough for him to take that one step across the line."

Evelyne was smiling at Malena, clearly ready to get started. Emily noticed, though, how every other head slowly turned toward Abbie. With Helen dead, they were automatically looking to her as their new leader, even if the position was still officially vacant.

Abbie nodded her head slowly, though she displayed none of the enthusiasm Evelyne was showing. "Very well. It's only nine o'clock. Shall we begin the search now?"

Serenity jumped up. "I'm going to get my books!"

Everyone else followed suit. As the witches trooped

upstairs, Emily beamed at Malena, who was already slowly flipping through the yellowed pages of her handwritten book. "Thank you," Emily said. "I'll go make a fresh batch of sweet tea."

By the time Emily returned to the dining room with a pitcher of tea and six glasses, everyone was seated around the table, working quietly. Piper was scribbling notes on a yellow legal pad as she consulted a worn paperback book. Serenity was holding a spiral notebook up in front of her face. The cover had red hearts drawn in marker all over it, and Emily wondered how young Serenity had been when she had started getting into witchcraft.

Abbie was typing on a laptop, and she glanced up in time to see Emily's surprised look. "We're modern witches!" Abbie said. "I went digital years ago."

Emily offered to pour the glasses of tea and bring them around so no one had to get up. Once everyone had been served, she quietly slipped out of the dining room and returned to the kitchen. She had intended to get the coffee maker prepared for breakfast the next morning, but instead, she sank down into a chair and rested her head on the kitchen table. The trip to the cemetery had gone by in such a blur that she hadn't had a moment to simply sit and absorb it all. She had seen Scott's ghost again, and he had seemed to appear at the sound of his mother's voice. Could Darlene help give him the boost he needed to get through the barrier? If everything Sage had told her about witches using energy to work their magic was true, then Emily felt hopeful they would find a way to help Scott before they returned the barrier to full strength on Sunday night.

"Please, please, please," Emily whispered.

Emily appreciated the solitude and the silence, and she felt both her mind and her shoulders beginning to relax when there was a sharp knock from the direction of the hallway. She sat up quickly. "Yes?"

No one was there, and when the knock sounded again, seeming to come from the wall next to the doorway, Emily became even more alert. "Mrs. Thompson, is something happening?"

One knock confirmed it.

"Is it Helen?"

In answer, a knock sounded again, but it was clearly in the hallway this time. Emily rose and walked toward the sound. As soon as she was in the hallway, there was another knock near the hall closet. Emily moved forward, but the knocking noises stayed one step ahead of her, leading her right back to the dining room.

The knocking ceased when Emily walked into the room, but she saw nothing amiss. Darlene and Malena were speaking in low voices to each other as Darlene gestured to a page in a book with color illustrations of plants. Piper was talking quietly to herself as she read a passage in her notebook. The others were silent as they pored through their reference material.

"Is she here?" Emily asked. Every witch glanced up, some of them looking startled. Clearly, they had been so absorbed in their research they had never heard Emily enter the room.

"Is who here?" Evelyne asked. Her eyes were darting around the room, and Emily suspected she already knew the answer to her own question.

"Mrs. Thompson, my former assistant, indicated Helen was in here," Emily clarified. "Do any of you sense her?"

Everyone held still. Darlene, Abbie, and Serenity all closed their eyes in concentration.

"Oh," Piper said in a worried voice. "It's cold. My back is freezing suddenly."

Emily looked at the spot behind Piper's chair, knowing a cold spot could indicate the presence of a ghost. She saw nothing out of the ordinary at first. Then, Emily realized the pen on the sideboard behind Piper was poised over a sheet of paper. It was moving slowly, and Emily blinked a few times, unsure if she was actually seeing the pen write on its own.

*Finally!* Emily thought joyfully. *I'm finally getting to see Kelly write a message!*

"Hold still, Piper," Emily said quietly. "Kelly is writing a message on the sideboard behind you."

"It's so cold," Piper said at the same time two loud knocks—Mrs. Thompson's way of saying *no*—sounded from the wall next to Emily.

"Are you disagreeing with me, Mrs. Thompson?" Emily asked.

*Knock.*

"It's not Kelly writing, then." Emily's joy immediately turned into disappointment as well as curiosity. "Is Helen the one writing a message?"

*Knock.*

The room became so silent Emily could hear the scratch of the pen against the sheet of paper. Everyone was watching, rapt, as Helen guided the pen with an invisible hand. After about two minutes, the pen suddenly fell, hitting the paper before rolling off the sideboard onto the floor.

Since Piper was the closest to the paper, she rose to retrieve it. As she lifted the sheet, she said, "I think she's gone now. I'm not cold anymore."

Everyone, including Emily, eagerly leaned forward to gaze at the paper as Piper placed it in the middle of the dining room table. Helen had scrawled strange symbols all over it, going over the lines again and again with the pen to make them dark and thick. Emily had no idea what the symbols meant, but the way Helen had drawn them, they felt angry.

"I've never seen these symbols before," Evelyne said.

"I have," Serenity said, her voice a nervous squeak. "They're symbols for working dark magic. Helen wants revenge on her killer."

# 12

Emily had never seen someone roll their eyes as dramatically as Abbie did in that moment. "Oh, please, Serenity," she said with an indignant sniff, "you've never so much as looked at the instructions for a dark spell, let alone worked one. How would you know what these symbols mean?"

Serenity's cheeks turned scarlet, and she looked away hastily. "I just know," she said, crossing her arms.

"It doesn't matter how she knows," Evelyne said. "Serenity is right. That symbol on the top left of the page is a heart with pins stuck in it. It's used to pierce the heart of the person you're working magic against."

Piper's mouth opened in surprise, and she stared at Evelyne, but she remained silent. Emily kept her own expression neutral, but she shared Piper's shock. Evelyne had denied working spells to bring bad luck to her coven, but she was clearly no stranger to dark magic.

"Until we learn which one of you killed Helen, we need protection." Abbie glared around at the other five witches.

"It could have been you," Piper grumbled. She ducked her head as Abbie's gaze fell on her.

"We need to conduct a binding spell to protect this house," Abbie continued, ignoring Piper.

"Whoa," Emily said, raising her hands in a warning gesture. "What's a binding spell?"

"It will prevent Helen from exerting her power and harming us," Abbie answered.

"Does this spell target just Helen or all of the ghosts here?"

Abbie was silent for a moment, and Emily took it to mean she didn't know the answer. Finally, Abbie said with a sneer, "Do you want to protect your guests or not?"

"I want to protect my guests *and* my ghosts. I won't allow anything that might hurt them." Emily lowered her hands, and she realized they were shaking. She knew Abbie wanted to keep her coven safe, but it felt like she was threatening the ghosts of Eternal Rest.

"Helen hasn't actually done any harm," Darlene said timidly.

"She's cursing us!" Serenity's voice was shrill.

"No, she's trying to get revenge on her killer," Evelyne corrected. "Maybe we should let justice be done."

Emily raised her hands again, this time to defend her guests rather than her ghosts. "Sage has already learned that Helen doesn't know who killed her, which means she might lash out at anyone. Abbie, I agree with you that protection measures are a smart idea, but I recommend using some kind of personal protection spell. Surely there's a way for all of you to be safe without involving my home or my ghosts."

*Deep breaths*, Emily told herself. Of all the trying guests she had ever had, none of them had ever challenged her quite the way these witches did.

As Emily focused on staying calm, the other women in the room began to argue. Emily tuned it out, not wanting any more of their drama. Apparently, neither did Abbie, because she clapped her hands loudly. "Enough! I have a personal protection spell we can all use on ourselves. Emily, I assume you have bay leaves and salt in your kitchen?"

"Of course."

"Please go get them for us. Sisters, go upstairs and grab any black tourmaline that you have."

All argument ceased as the witches rushed to do as Abbie instructed. With a little shrug, Emily went to the kitchen and retrieved a small container of bay leaves and a box of sea salt. As Emily returned to the dining room with them, Abbie was tearing sheets of paper out of a small notebook, placing one sheet in front of each chair.

Not wanting to seem like some kind of curious tourist, Emily put the bay leaves and salt down on the dining room table and retreated into the parlor. She shut the door behind her and called softly, "Kelly? Mrs. Thompson? Grandma Gray, are you there?"

The knock on the wall above Emily's desk seemed to confirm that the Eternal Rest ghosts were in the parlor with Emily. "Do you all understand that the spell each witch is about to do is for their safety? It's not about you. It's about Helen's ghost."

Another knock sounded, quieter this time.

Emily sighed and paced to the front windows. She pulled back the side of one curtain and looked at the darkness beyond the glow of the front porch light. She had once told Trevor she felt trapped at Eternal Rest, but now that analogy seemed to have become reality. Yes, she could leave if she wanted, but she would have to pass the police officers on duty to do so. Emily couldn't see them since they were beyond the reach of the light, but she knew they were there, keeping watch on Eternal Rest.

When Emily turned and walked back to her desk, Kelly had written a note in a small, timid hand: *We feel unsafe. Threatened. Not by guests but the ghost. Dark, dark, dark.*

Emily had offered up all the soothing words she could remember her mother saying to her when she had woken up from nightmares as a child. She wanted to reassure not just Kelly and her other ghosts, but herself, as well.

Finally, shortly before midnight, the witches went upstairs. Emily glanced in the dining room as she headed to her bedroom and saw they had left their research scattered across the table.

Relieved to be alone—truly alone without having to worry a guest could walk through the door at any moment —Emily slipped off her shoes and tipped forward onto her bed. She lay there on her stomach, her face cradled in her arms and her feet dangling off the edge. At some point, she fell asleep just like that.

Emily thought she was having one of those childhood nightmares later, when she heard a loud, high-pitched blaring. She clamped her hands over her ears and twisted around so she was on her back.

Slowly, Emily realized the sound wasn't part of a dream. She was awake, her bedroom light was on, and she was still dressed.

*Then what is making that awful sound? Is Helen's ghost doing that?*

As Emily sat up, the fog of sleep finally lifted, and she jumped to her feet. She didn't even bother to put her shoes on before she threw open her bedroom door and bolted down the hallway.

Emily quickly punched in the code to turn off her security alarm. She had set it before bed, just in case one of her guests tried to make a run for it in the middle of the night.

The front door was already unlocked, and Emily rushed outside. The two police officers guarding the front of the house were running toward the porch as Emily hurried down the steps. A figure stood between them, though Emily couldn't tell who it was. The person seemed to be wearing a dark hood of some kind.

Two hands shot up in surrender. "It's okay! I'm not doing anything wrong!"

"Piper?" Emily asked, recognizing the voice.

Slowly, Piper turned around. She was wearing a hooded black cardigan. Her frizzed hair glowed around her head like a halo in the porch light as she lowered the hood. "I'm just going to the cemetery. Honest. I didn't know the security alarm was set."

"So you were just going to make a run for it while the alarm went off?" one of the officers asked.

Piper was still facing Emily, a pleading look on her face as she answered, "I need to go to the cemetery! Please. I have to collect graveyard dirt, and I need to do it under the light of a waxing moon." Piper pointed toward the horizon, where a nearly full moon was gliding just above the tree line.

Emily bit her lip, trying to decide if she believed Piper or not. She shut her eyes, took a deep breath, and focused. Even with her eyes closed, she could sense where Piper was standing. There was a feeling of desperation rolling off her. Emily got the distinct impression Piper really had snuck out of the house to go to the cemetery, and not to run away under cover of night.

*Sage will be happy to know I'm putting my skills to use,* Emily thought briefly. She opened her eyes again and peered over Piper's shoulder toward the shadowed forms of the police officers. "It's okay," she told them. "I'll escort Piper to the cemetery." Emily quickly realized that although she believed Piper's story, the woman could still very well have been the one who had killed Helen, so she added, "However, I know we're not supposed to roam around on our own, so could one of you please come with us?"

Piper looked at Emily gratefully. "Thank you."

Emily nodded and told Piper to sit tight while she went inside to get some things. By then, the rest of her guests were huddled at the top of the stairs, slightly panicked expressions on each of their faces.

"Piper is missing!" Malena cried.

"No, she's out front. It's fine," Emily said reassuringly. "She wanted to step out for a bit, and she didn't know the security alarm was set."

"She was trying to escape, wasn't she?" Evelyne sounded like she was near hysterics. "I never would have suspected her of killing someone. Piper seems too straight-laced for that!"

Emily waved a hand quickly. "No, she wasn't trying to get away. She wanted to take a walk." Emily wasn't sure why she felt the need to hide Piper's true reason for leaving the house. She just knew it felt like something that needed to be kept secret, at least for the moment. "I'm going to go with her, and so is a police officer. Please, ladies, go back to bed. There's nothing to worry about."

*Except who among us is a murderer.*

After finally convincing the other witches to go back to bed and putting on her shoes, Emily returned to the front yard with a flashlight and the key to the cemetery. As she and Piper began to walk across the grass toward the front gate of Hilltop, Emily spoke quietly so the officer following them wouldn't overhear. "My friend Reed, who's the sexton here, once gave me graveyard dirt for spiritual protection. Is that why you want it, too?"

"Yes. And it doesn't have to be gathered under a waxing moon, but it does help. Plus, I didn't want the others to know what I was doing."

"I figured as much. Why else would you be sneaking

out to do it?" Emily gave a short laugh. "I'm a light sleeper, you know. I'm amazed I didn't hear the stairs creaking."

"I have a basset hound who howls if you wake him up in the middle of the night," Piper said. "I've learned to be as quiet as a mouse."

"Why don't you want the others to know what you're doing? Abbie insisted on everyone performing a protection spell against Helen's anger, so I don't see why adding to it with graveyard dirt would need to be a secret."

Piper sighed. "They would either laugh at me or think I must have a guilty conscience."

"The guilty conscience part I understand," Emily said carefully. "After all, somebody here killed Helen, and it would make sense that whomever did it would be especially worried about a vengeful spirit. But I don't understand why your coven would laugh at you."

"They would laugh because the truth would sound so ridiculous to them. I've never told any of them, but I think Helen was working dark magic against me when she was still alive. Those symbols she drew tonight, I've seen a couple of them before. Helen may not know who killed her, but that just means she might lash out at all of us. I don't want to be under the influence of her dark magic again."

Helen had apparently been working magic against Evelyne, and here Piper was, accusing Helen of working dark magic against her. If Helen had been after Evelyne's spot as coven leader, Emily could see how she might have gotten carried away in her eagerness to be in charge. Piper, though, hadn't struck Emily as competition for Helen.

"Why would Helen want to work dark magic against you?" Emily asked.

"Because," Piper said flatly, "I got the life she had wanted for her daughter. I married the man Helen had always wanted her daughter to marry."

"Carrie was seven years younger than me," Piper continued. "She and Owen had known each other for most of their lives, and they even dated for a short while in high school. Helen liked that he was rich, of course. But, Owen and I met through work, and we just hit it off. It didn't matter that I was older. We got married just a year after we started dating."

"How long have you two been married?"

"Twelve years now."

"And you think Helen worked dark magic against you to get revenge? Was she trying to kill you?"

"Kill me? Goodness, I don't think so! I think she wanted Owen and I to get divorced. That way, I'd be unhappy, and Carrie would have another shot at him."

"Poor Owen," Emily mumbled. The guy had never asked to be at the center of a witch dispute.

"I was gardening one day, and I found a leather pouch in the front yard. We use them a lot in witchcraft, but usually for good things. You fill them with the right objects and herbs for, say, getting money or being happy, and they act as a focusing tool for bringing those things into your life. The one I found, though, had a piece of paper with a symbol on it. Helen drew that same symbol tonight. It's a circle that looks like it has a triangle sticking in one side. It's the symbol for driving a wedge between people."

Emily had been unlocking the cemetery gate as Piper spoke, but she stopped abruptly and looked at Piper. "Maybe that symbol tonight wasn't directed at you. Well, not just at you. Maybe Helen wants to drive a wedge between everyone in the coven. She knows you're weaker individually."

Piper slowly swung her flashlight in an arc, the beam tracing a circle in the grass as she thought. "Maybe you're right. If we're all arguing and accusing each other, the truth is bound to come out faster. She was a smart lady, even if she was a total—"

The squeak of the iron gate as Emily pushed it open drowned out Piper's last word.

"Where do you want to do this?" Emily asked.

"I'd prefer an open patch, so the moon is actually shining on the ground." Piper moved toward the left. She only went about twenty feet inside the cemetery before she stopped and said, "Here, this will do nicely."

The plot belonged to the Sinclair family. Emily knew, even without needing to read the epitaphs, that Frederick Sinclair had emigrated to the United States from a small village in Scotland back in 1847. He had settled in Oak Hill, married, started the town's first brick manufacturing company, then died in 1892. From everything Emily had ever read about Frederick, he had been a good, honest businessman and a kind husband and father. It seemed like a perfect plot for collecting graveyard dirt.

Emily gave Piper her full approval, telling her she had picked a good plot, then stepped back. She wasn't sure if Piper would just fill up a box or if there was some ritual that needed to be done. Either way, she felt like she ought to give the witch some privacy.

While Piper worked, Emily chatted quietly with the

police officer, whose name was Darren. "I'm fairly new to the force," he said, his eyes shining in the moonlight, "but I've already heard that you're Detective Hernandez's favorite witness."

Emily pursed her lips but refrained from saying anything.

Piper soon announced she was finished, so the three of them walked back to the house. Emily wished Darren a good night, then she and Piper went inside. "I'm setting the security alarm again," Emily said quietly. "If you decide you need to go out in the middle of the night for more graveyard dirt, come let me know."

"I promise. Thank you, Emily."

"You're welcome. I hope the graveyard dirt helps."

Piper crept up the stairs without making a sound, and Emily had to concede she had been right about her ability to be silent. It wasn't even two o'clock in the morning yet, so Emily took the time to put on her pajamas and wash her face before she went to bed. This time, she was properly under the covers instead of sprawled on top of them.

Emily flicked off the nightstand light, but as she blinked a few times in the sudden darkness, there seemed to be something blocking her view from the bed to the walnut wardrobe across the room. As her eyes adjusted, Emily could see there was a concentration of darkness at the foot of her bed. None of the moonlight coming through the window or the faint glow from her alarm clock illuminated the shape.

The room around Emily continued to come into focus, dim but clear. Her dresser, the pile of books she planned to read someday, and the photos on the wall were all visible. Still, though, the darkness at the foot of the bed remained. It seemed to be in the shape of a human.

Just as Emily reached for her lamp again, a woman's

low, angry voice spoke. Emily didn't understand the words, but she thought they sounded like Latin.

Light flared through the room when Emily turned on the lamp, but the form was gone. She threw the covers back and got out of bed, looking for it. She even knelt down and peeked under the bed, but no one was there. It had been Helen's voice, but why was the woman's ghost appearing to Emily? And what had been those strange words she was uttering?

Without hesitation, Emily threw a bathrobe on over her pajamas and sprinted as quietly as she could to the parlor. Once she had turned on every lamp in the room, she shut the door and sat at her desk. She typed out what she had heard Helen say, spelling the words phonetically. The second word Helen had said had sounded like *magic* but with a long *a* on the end.

*She was saying something about magic.*

Once she had written down the four words as best she could remember—and spell—them, Emily went online and found a Latin translator. It took her half an hour of trying different spellings, but finally she had Helen's words exactly as they had been spoken: *Speculum magiae, malum reflecte.* "Magic mirror, reflect the evil," Emily murmured. Rather than feeling frightened, she sat back in her chair with a frustrated huff. "Not another haunted mirror!"

Not knowing what else to do, or what Helen's ghost had meant with those words, Emily went back to bed. She left her nightstand lamp on this time.

The next morning, Emily was yawning as she sat once again in the parlor. She had already set breakfast on the sideboard in the dining room, and she was nursing her third cup of coffee. When she heard her guests coming downstairs, she waited about ten minutes before joining them as they ate. She figured they deserved to have some coffee and croissants before she shared the news about her encounter with Helen.

The witches were already bent over their books and notes as they ate. "Good morning, ladies," Emily said from the doorway. The responses were polite but subdued. "Helen stopped by my bedroom last night."

That generated a much more animated response. Suddenly, Emily had six pairs of eyes staring at her. Serenity froze, her coffee cup lifted to her lips.

"I went back to bed last night, after Piper and I returned to the house," Emily explained. "Just after I turned off the light, I could see a dark, human-shaped shadow at the foot of my bed. I heard a voice, and I'm almost certain it was Helen's. She said something in Latin, and it translated to 'magic mirror, reflect this evil.' Do you think she's working magic with one of the mirrors in the house?"

The witches looked at each other. "What were the Latin words, exactly?" Evelyne asked.

When Emily began to repeat Helen's words verbatim, Serenity stood quickly, her coffee sloshing over the rim of the cup and onto her notebook. "No! Don't say them out loud. Write them down. When you speak words, you give them power."

"Oh. Okay." Emily wrote *speculum magiae, malum reflecte* on the notepad Darlene offered her.

"I don't think Helen was referring to a physical mirror," Abbie said after a moment of studying the text. "I assume this is more figurative. She wants the evil that was inflicted on her to be reflected back on the one who's responsible."

"I think Abbie is right," Serenity said. "She wants her killer to be killed. This is revenge magic."

Emily shifted uncomfortably from one foot to the other. "Why did she come to me to say those words? Does she think I killed her? Was she trying to curse me?" Emily could feel her heart pounding against her chest, and she had to remind herself it was from fear and not because Helen's ghost was trying to give her a heart attack.

"You mentioned that you're developing your skills as a psychic medium," Darlene pointed out. "Helen can probably sense that, which is why she appeared to you. She knew you were the most likely person to hear her message."

Emily decided she liked that explanation a whole lot better. Still, Helen's words had a sinister implication. "She wanted to give a warning to whomever killed her. A couple of you have mentioned Helen might have been dabbling in dark magic, and Sage got the same impression. Do you think that's what this is?"

Serenity sighed and shook her head sadly. "Helen wanted our coven to delve into magic that crossed the line between good and evil."

"Serenity!" Abbie said sharply.

"Emily deserves to know! She's stuck in this mess, too. Helen's leadership tactics were as ruthless as her magic. It's no wonder she was killed." Serenity stood and paced angrily to the front windows.

"What kind of magic did she want your coven to do?" Emily asked.

"Eliminating competition for promotions at work, bringing bad luck to people who didn't treat us well, that sort of thing. Nothing murderous, but still spiteful." Malena's voice was quiet and sad.

*Except Helen's magic was murderous, at least toward Evelyne,* Emily thought.

Darlene, Piper, and Evelyne stirred uncomfortably as Malena fell quiet, and Emily wondered how many times Helen had convinced the coven to actually perform those spells. Her thoughts went back to her conversation with

Piper the night before, and suddenly, the idea of Helen working dark magic against Piper seemed a lot more plausible. "Helen was interested in spiteful spells, like trying to break up marriages," Emily said quietly.

Evelyne's eyes flicked to Piper. "We didn't help her with that," she said firmly.

"Helen wasn't a bad person, or a bad witch," Abbie said angrily. "The woman was just killed, and you're all turning on her. She was our coven leader, and you should respect her, even in death. Shame on all of you! Helen wanted us all to get ahead in life, and sometimes, that meant getting competition out of the way or sending a message that we are not women to cross. There is nothing wrong with that kind of magic."

"Of course you would say that!" Serenity said bitingly as she turned away from the front windows and faced Abbie. Her face no longer looked like a fairy's. Her eyebrows drew together, and her mouth twisted in disgust. "You and Helen were cut from the same cloth. You're probably already working spells to make sure you're the next coven leader."

"And why wouldn't I be?" Abbie said, rising. "Helen has been grooming me for the position for the past three years. Of course I'm the best witch to lead this coven."

"Maybe you killed Helen because you were tired of waiting for the job," Evelyne said snidely.

Abbie rounded on Evelyne. "Oh, you're one to point the finger. Maybe you killed her so you could take the position back!"

Evelyne stood. "How dare you!"

Emily instinctively took a step backward. Not only did she not want to be around the arguing and accusations, but as the tensions and voices had risen in the room, so had the feeling that something was about to happen. It was the same rubber band feeling Emily had sensed in the cemetery, right before the dark entity holding Scott captive had appeared and lunged at her. Emily didn't want to be in the room when the rubber band snapped.

But it was too late. Before she could turn and leave the room, there was a scraping sound. Emily looked up just in time to see an antique vase slide across the fireplace mantel before it went airborne. It sailed just inches from Abbie's face and shattered against the wall next to Emily.

As the vase had flown through the air, Emily had instinctively brought her arms up and turned her face away. She actually felt small shards of porcelain spray against her left arm as the vase shattered against the wall.

Someone screamed, and then everything fell silent. The tension in the room had changed. Emily no longer felt it in a paranormal sense: Helen's energy had built up and been discharged. Instead, it was the tension between the witches that had shifted. The rift between them had grown now that accusations of murder were being said out loud. Evelyne was eyeing Abbie with a mixture of fear and anger, Piper simply looked terrified, and Darlene shook her head, her lips pressed tightly together as she looked around the table with a disapproving glare.

"Well," Serenity said quietly, "I guess Helen wants us to stop fighting. Abbie, I'm sorry I yelled at you. I'm scared, and I'm upset."

Abbie's head jerked toward Serenity, and her mouth opened like she was going to retort. Instead, her face and shoulders relaxed, and for the first time since Helen's death, Emily saw what looked like real sorrow on Abbie's beautiful face. "We're all scared and upset," she said. "I'm sure none of us meant the things we said."

When Abbie looked around at the other witches, there

was a clear challenge in her gaze. She was silently daring Evelyne to say she had meant it when she had accused Abbie of killing Helen.

"I think we all need to cool off," Piper said. "We need to be united for the ritual this weekend, and all we're doing is making that symbol Helen drew come true. We don't need magic to drive a wedge between us, because we're doing it to ourselves. Let's split up so we can meditate, work a mood-booster spell, or do whatever we each need to do to calm down."

"That's the most level-headed thing anyone has said this morning," Darlene said, rising. She walked to the sideboard and poured herself another cup of coffee. "I'm going to sit in the tent and let nature soothe me."

"Me, too," Serenity said.

The other four witches went upstairs to their rooms, leaving Emily to clean up the broken shards of porcelain. She wanted to lecture Helen about breaking antiques, but she figured it wouldn't do much good.

Emily loaded the breakfast dishes into the dishwasher and cleaned the coffee maker, then grabbed a leftover biscuit before she retreated to the parlor. As she sat at her desk, she heard the front door open and close, followed by a quiet knock on the open parlor door.

Emily turned around in her chair and saw Darlene there, a concerned look on her face. "Emily, I'm so sorry about this morning. Like I said, we haven't always been like this."

"You haven't always accused each other of murder, you mean?" Emily had meant to say it teasingly, but it didn't come out that way.

"At each other's throats. Jealous, suspicious. Maybe Helen's leadership was more toxic than I realized." Darlene sank down in one of the wingback chairs, then chuckled softly. "I didn't come down here to complain, though. I actually came to check on you. You've got a lot on your shoulders: you're trying to help Scott, and you're hosting a murderer at your B and B."

Emily moved from her desk chair to the second wing-back chair, which was on the opposite end of the coffee table and across from Darlene. "And I have a very angry ghost haunting my home. Darlene, do you think you could teach me that personal protection spell y'all did yesterday? I don't want to be vulnerable to Helen's ire, either."

Darlene nodded. "I totally understand you wanting to do that, especially after she visited you last night. However, I don't think you're in danger from her."

"She threw a vase at my head."

"I don't think she did. That vase got a lot closer to hitting Abbie than you, but I know—er, knew—Helen. If she had wanted to hit someone, she would have. I think she was simply trying to scare all of us. Actually, I think you should try to communicate with Helen. If she came to you because she knows you can sense her better than any of us, then maybe there's more she wants to say."

"I can try. Will you stay here with me, just in case I need help?" Emily didn't like the idea of talking to Helen, but she had to concede Darlene had a point.

"Of course. You do what you need to do, and I'll keep an eye on you."

Emily sat up straight, placed her hands on her thighs, and closed her eyes. She pictured Helen in her mind. "Helen," Emily said quietly. "Are you there? Do you want to come talk to me or show me something?"

For a few minutes, nothing happened. Then, slowly, the air around Emily began to grow cold. "That's good, Helen. I can feel your presence. I'm listening."

In response, the air simply grew colder, until Emily felt goosebumps on her arms. She shivered and ran her hands briskly against her skin. Distantly, she could hear the gentle sound of Darlene breathing, her inhales and exhales sounding almost meditative.

"What do you want to tell me?" Emily prompted Helen.

Emily focused on listening. Instead of hearing Helen's voice like she had in her bedroom, Emily heard only silence. She realized with a start that it was more than just the absence of a ghost talking to her. She could no longer hear the sound of Darlene's breathing.

"Please, Helen. I need you to speak to me or show me something. The silence doesn't make any sense to me." Emily was leaning slightly forward now, listening for any little sound, but none came. The cold and the silence persisted.

Vaguely, Emily felt something against her shoulder. She blinked her eyes open and saw Darlene standing in front of her, one hand gripping Emily tightly. Darlene's eyes were wide as they searched Emily's face. "Are you okay?" Darlene asked frantically.

"Yes, I'm fine. Why?" Emily noticed she could now hear footsteps upstairs, and the cold had disappeared.

"The doorbell rang, but you didn't respond to it at all. I called your name twice, and when you didn't answer me, I panicked."

"Someone's at the door?" Emily shook her head in confusion. "I was listening so hard, but it was just silence. I never heard the doorbell or you."

Darlene let go of Emily's arm. "You were able to contact Helen?"

"I felt icy cold. Helen was definitely here, but she didn't speak to me, and I don't know what she was trying to communicate." Emily rose. "I guess I should answer the door."

Emily felt like her feet weighed one hundred pounds each as she trudged to the door. Connecting with Helen's ghost hadn't accomplished anything other than draining Emily's energy. That, and making her feel even more scared. Despite Darlene's reassurances that Helen wouldn't have Emily on her vengeance list, Emily still felt uncomfortable.

It was Danny Hernandez at the door, and he smiled politely at Emily. "I'm afraid I need to take you downtown for some formalities," he said. "Your guests will have to survive without you for a bit."

"That might be harder than you realize," Emily said, throwing a wary glance over her shoulder. "Helen has already thrown a vase across the room today, and it's quite possible she's trying to curse her coven."

Danny's smile disappeared. "It sounds like I've missed some excitement. If things are getting dangerous here, then that's even more reason to get you out of the house. Come on. I'll drive us."

Reluctantly, Emily retrieved her purse and told Darlene to call her if she or the others needed anything. Or, Emily added, if Helen started acting up again. She had no idea what Danny could need her at the police station for. As soon as they were in his truck, she said, "I don't think I have any helpful information that you don't already know. What kind of formalities do you need me for?"

Danny turned onto the two-lane road in the direction of downtown. He was smiling again, but this time, it was mischievous instead of polite. "Your guests are confined to Eternal Rest, not you. I didn't want them to get jealous if I told you the real reason we're heading to town. I'm taking you to lunch."

"Oh." Emily was surprised, but beyond that, she couldn't decide if she appreciated the gesture or found it annoying, because it meant she couldn't be at home to keep an eye on her guests.

"It's not fair for you to be stuck there. You didn't

murder anyone. Well, not that I know of." Danny threw Emily a sly look.

Emily just gave Danny a tight-lipped smile in return, and he quickly sobered. "What's wrong?"

"Helen's ghost has communicated with me twice since last night, and both times have been a little scary."

"I'm sorry she scared you, but it sounds like you're really making progress with your psychic abilities. That's great, Emily."

"It is," Emily said with a shrug. At the moment, it was hard for her to get excited about her growth when it was resulting in such unsettling experiences. She would much rather talk to nice ghosts, like Mrs. Thompson.

Danny drove to The Depot, which sat on the square in downtown Oak Hill. Since it was summer and a Saturday, the square was filled with traffic and pedestrians. It was mostly out-of-town visitors, no doubt, there for a day of antique shopping. Danny had to search for a parking spot, finally finding one a block behind The Depot.

The restaurant was just as busy as the square, but there was one small table on the patio that had just been vacated. As she sat down, Emily had to admit the change of scenery was nice. Helen's ghost surely wouldn't have followed her downtown, so she didn't have to worry about her own safety for a while. And, even though there was only a little shade from a nearby dogwood tree, the heat actually felt nice after the bitter cold Emily had felt radiating off Helen.

As they ate, Emily caught Danny up on everything that had happened since she had last seen him. As she wrapped up, she was surprised to realize how much had happened in just twenty-four hours. "I've said it before, but I mean it more than ever: I need a vacation after we solve this murder," she concluded.

"I'm afraid lunch is all I can offer at the moment," Danny said, winking at Emily.

After the stress of the past few days, Emily felt zero guilt about ordering dessert after she finished her sandwich. She got a hot fudge sundae, which was brought to her by Jay, the owner of The Depot. He wanted to get the latest Oak Hill gossip right from the source. When Danny realized Emily's ice cream was melting as she answered one question after another from Jay, he took over the storytelling while Emily gratefully turned her attention to her sundae.

Once they were finished with lunch, Emily expected Danny to take her right back to Eternal Rest. She began to walk in the direction of his truck, but Danny took Emily gently by the arm and steered her toward the square instead. "One more stop," he said. "Sage asked us to visit."

Seeing Beyond was in an Art Deco office building just a couple blocks off the square, and it was a short walk there, though Emily and Danny had to dodge the tourists and shoppers clogging the sidewalks. Sage was sitting at her huge oak desk when they walked in, and she didn't look up from her laptop as she said, "Sit down, you two. I just need a minute."

Emily and Danny had just settled onto the midnight-blue velvet of the Victorian sofa that served as a client waiting area when Sage shut her laptop with a bang and rose. She walked toward Emily and stood in front of her, her face somber. "I dreamed about it last night, Em. The dark entity. It can't get through the barrier yet, but it's able to send its thoughts through. It looked just like it did when we saw it in that meadow. Dark, dense. I think it was taunting me because it's so confident it can break through the barrier soon."

Emily reached up and took her friend's hand. "Oh, Sage, I'm so sorry."

"Do you remember how frigid the air was when we encountered the entity at the lake? I woke up freezing just like I did that day."

Emily gasped and squeezed Sage's hand. "Oh, no," she groaned. "The cold, the silence. How did I not recognize the signs? I don't think it was Helen's ghost I was communicating with earlier!"

# 15

Sage bent forward at the waist until she was eye-to-eye with Emily. "Tell me every single detail."

Emily did just that, beginning with Helen's strange visit to her bedroom the previous night. When she was done, Sage made a swatting motion, indicating Emily should scoot toward Danny. Once Emily complied, Sage squeezed in next to Emily. Three people on the sofa was a tight fit, and Emily was conscious of the way her left shoulder and leg were pressed against Danny's body.

"First of all, I don't think that was the actual entity," Sage said thoughtfully. "If it were able to get through the barrier already, I think it would have done something a lot more dramatic than the same old cold and silence. Second, way to go, Em! I'm so happy you're embracing your abilities and trying to make contact with ghosts."

"Even though it might have been the wrong ghost," Emily grumbled.

"Maybe you did communicate with the essence of that entity. It could also have been Helen, though. Cold spots indicate ghosts, so that part of your experience could have been her simply standing near you."

"And the silence?"

Emily felt Sage's shoulder move against hers in a shrugging motion. "That isn't as easy to answer, though it almost sounds like you were in a trance."

"Helen hypnotizing me is almost as creepy as the idea of the entity visiting me." Emily shuddered. Danny's cell phone rang, and Emily jumped in surprise. *Silly*, she told herself.

Danny rose and answered the call, walking toward a window while Sage continued speaking. "I don't think she hypnotized you. Rather, I think you might have been so focused that you slipped into a psychic trance, almost like your mind went into a void between this world and the spirit world."

"I didn't even know that was possible. It's a good thing, I guess?"

"Actually, yes. It takes a lot of mediums years to learn how to reach that state. You did it by complete accident."

Emily opened her mouth to reply, but before she could speak, she heard Danny say incredulously, "Are you kidding me?" She and Sage looked over at him. He was still on his phone, and he was pacing angrily in front of the window. "Yeah, yeah. You have a point."

Sage and Emily exchanged a look, their eyebrows raised, as Danny added, "Emily is with me. I'll bring her," and hung up.

"What's wrong?" Emily and Sage asked in unison as Danny turned toward them.

"Nothing is wrong. However, we aren't going back to Eternal Rest just yet. We're actually going to the funeral home."

"Yeah, because what I want to see is more dead bodies," Emily said sarcastically.

"While we were investigating Helen's murder on Thursday night, the witches requested permission to perform a death ritual for Helen. Her family has granted permission, so the coven is going to the funeral home right now." Danny's initial surprise had clearly faded, and he was beginning to look excited.

"Danny, that's insane!" Emily said. "One of those women murdered Helen, and you're letting them go on a field trip to see her body?"

"Actually, this could be just what this case needs. What an interesting chance for me to observe the suspects. They're performing a ritual over the victim, and I get to sit back and watch how each one of them handles it."

Emily could only shake her head at how ridiculous it all seemed, even though she could understand Danny's enthusiasm. Sage made Emily promise to tell her all about it later, and she even suggested Emily film some of the ritual on her cell phone.

"Ew, no," Emily said, horrified. "Don't worry, though, you'll get your own chance to watch the witches in action soon enough. They're looking for a way to help Scott get through the barrier before they strengthen it tomorrow night, and they said they'll likely need your mediumship skills to do it."

Sage spread her hands. "I'm not sure I can do much, but you know I'll try. My energy reserves are low, but maybe you and I can join psychic forces to bring Scott through."

With that hope in her mind, Emily hugged Sage before she and Danny left for what Emily was sure would be a surreal afternoon.

J.D. Bonim and Sons Funeral Home had always fascinated Emily. With tall columns across a wide front porch and a widow's walk atop the third story, it looked more like a New England mansion to her than a place to prepare bodies for burial. Its size and architectural style stuck out in the small North Georgia town, but Emily had to admit it was beautiful. Emily's grandparents, like most residents of Oak Hill, had been brought to J.D. Bonim and Sons after their deaths.

So had Scott.

*At least,* Emily told herself as she and Danny walked up the wide marble steps to the front porch, *I'm not here this time for my husband.* Nevertheless, Emily felt a heaviness in her chest as she remembered the awful trips to the funeral home to make Scott's funeral and burial arrangements.

The six living witches were all seated in one of the small viewing rooms to the left of the reception area. A police officer was standing watch at the door, and he opened it for Danny and Emily. Soft lighting illuminated floral wallpaper and rows of chairs with burgundy seats. Three of the witches sat in the front row, and the other three sat behind them, leaning forward so they could all whisper together. As Emily and Danny entered the room, the chatter ceased.

"Don't mind us, ladies," Danny said. "I'm just here to keep an eye on Helen."

Six pairs of eyes narrowed judgmentally at that, as if the witches felt like Danny suspected them of wanting to desecrate the body. Danny just flashed a bright smile and retreated to the back of the room, where he put his hands in the pockets of his black pants and leaned against the wall.

"And let me know if you need anything," Emily said awkwardly to her guests.

"Just silence," Abbie said pointedly.

Emily nodded and turned to join Danny at the back of the room. "But thank you for coming," Serenity called softly after her.

Just a few minutes later, an elderly man in an olive-green suit wheeled a casket on a gurney through a side door. The casket was pale blue, and the steel hardware on it gleamed in the overhead lights. The man in the suit navigated the gurney to the open space in front of the chairs, then lifted the casket lid. Emily walked forward a short way, and even from so far back, she could see how good Helen looked. She was wearing a lilac dress, and her gray hair was neatly styled in soft waves. The man nodded at the women and retreated back through the side door.

As one, the witches rose and walked forward to crowd around Helen's body. Someone sniffed loudly, and Emily watched as Darlene put a comforting arm around Malena's shoulders. After a few minutes, Serenity said in a wavering voice, "Okay, sisters. Let's begin. Evelyne, please place the candles around Helen and light them. Piper, please get the veil ready. Malena and Darlene, you two stand over on the other side of Helen. Abbie and I will stay on this side."

The witches began to silently follow Serenity's orders, and Emily was surprised she was the one taking charge instead of Abbie.

Soon, there was a ring of white candles balanced around the edge of the casket. Abbie turned off the lights, so only the glow from the flames illuminated the room. Serenity began speaking softly, her words not reaching Emily, but her tone rising and falling rhythmically. Piper leaned forward and draped a length of white lace over Helen. Emily watched nervously, expecting the lace to come into contact with one of the candles at any moment, but Piper moved slowly and carefully. Soon, the lace was draped from Helen's feet to the top of her head.

When smoke began to rise from somewhere around Helen's knees, Emily stiffened, immediately thinking the lace had, in fact, caught on fire. In a few moments, though, a strong, earthy scent drifted to the back of the room, and Emily knew it was just incense.

The witches held hands, making a circle around the casket as they joined Serenity in the chanting. Emily caught the words "transition" and "journey" in the soft, strangely soothing sound.

Emily leaned back against the wall and felt herself relaxing. The darkness, the smell of the incense, and the chanting washed over her, and the anxiousness she had felt walking into the funeral home disappeared. She still didn't know all of the words the witches were saying, but she could feel the sentiment: death wasn't an ending, but the next stage of existence. The witches wanted Helen to have a smooth journey, but Emily's thoughts were on Scott, and how she wanted to get him back on the correct course for his own trip through the afterlife.

*We will help you, Scott. I know we will. Between these women, me, and Sage, we will have the knowledge and the energy to pull you through the barrier.*

It was a peace and surety Emily hadn't felt since before Scott's car crash, and she closed her eyes to enjoy the feeling. It was interrupted by a frustrated sigh from Danny, who leaned toward her and whispered, "This isn't helping at all. Not one of them is acting strangely."

Emily reluctantly opened her eyes. Danny was right: each woman seemed to be fully committed to the ritual, and not one of them looked nervous or angry or any of the other emotions Emily expected a murderer to show when confronted with the body of their victim. The witches had begun moving slowly in a clockwise motion around the casket, and as Emily watched their faces slowly drift past in the candlelight, she saw nothing but concentration on each one.

With her own little sigh, Emily sat down in a nearby chair and folded her arms on the back of the chair in front of her. She put her forehead on her arms and tried to recapture that feeling of peace. Instead, her mind went back to worrying how they could possibly help Scott by the next evening.

The chanting began to rise in volume, and Emily could finally understand the words. "Let her find the path of peace as she walks in the world of undying spirit." The witches said the phrase three times, and then there was silence. Emily lifted her head to see the witches standing still, their hands still clasped and their heads bowed.

"The ritual is complete," Serenity said solemnly. She lifted her face toward the ceiling. "Helen, I hope you find your way."

Piper turned on the lights as Evelyne blew out the candles. The witches still lingered next to the casket, but now they simply looked like grieving women at a viewing.

The man in the green suit returned, but instead of removing the casket, he looked around the room until his eyes landed on Danny. He pointed at the door Danny and Emily had come through and jerked his chin toward it. Danny and Emily quietly exited through the door, the reception area seeming blindingly bright after the dim lights inside the room.

The man came out of another door to meet them. His silver hair shone in the sunshine streaming through the front windows, and he had keen dark eyes behind his wire-rim glasses. "Detective Hernandez, it's good to see you!" The man reached out to shake Danny's hand. "And Mrs. Buchanan, you worked with my son, I believe, when you were here after your own loss. I'm J.D. Bonim, Junior."

Emily shook the man's hand as he continued, "My daddy, J.D. Senior, started this place in nineteen fifty-three. We've had a number of your people come through here, Mrs. Buchanan."

"Just Emily is fine, Mr. Bonim." Emily wasn't sure if she was appalled at the man's casual talk of her dead relatives or relieved by how natural he made it sound.

"And you can just call me J.D." The man lowered his voice and said, "There's something I wanted to talk to you about, Detective. I was going to stop by the police station, but then I found out you'd be here. When we prepared Mrs. Harper this morning, we found a small piece of paper that had been folded and shoved under her watch-band. It was completely hidden between the band and her wrist, and it fell out when we removed her watch. I put it in a plastic bag in case you want to dust it for fingerprints. Here."

J.D. pulled the bag out of his suit pocket. Inside was a small square of parchment paper, no larger than a match-book. Emily and Danny both leaned toward it and squinted.

It was covered with the same symbols Helen's ghost had drawn on the paper in the dining room.

16

"I don't understand," Emily said. "Why would Helen draw these symbols, then tuck the paper in her watchband? When her ghost drew these symbols in the dining room, Serenity said she thought Helen was working dark magic to get revenge on whomever killed her, but she obviously did this before she died. Helen's ghost has indicated she doesn't know who actually killed her, so it doesn't make sense she would have targeted the person before her murder."

"Ghost?" J.D. looked at Emily with an amused smile. "I've heard the stories of your haunted B and B, but I didn't realize you actually believe in ghosts!"

"Are you a skeptic?" Emily asked.

"Oh, of course," J.D. answered slyly. "We don't ever have strange activity here at J.D. Bonim and Sons. At least, that's what we tell our patrons when they inquire." He grinned at Emily.

"Thanks for passing this along to me," Danny said, carefully taking the plastic bag from J.D. "I think it's time to have a long chat with these witches about the symbols and what they mean."

As Danny and Emily wished J.D. a nice afternoon and said goodbye, the witches filed out of the room. The police officer guarding the door began to walk with them, telling

Danny he was going to take the women back to Eternal Rest. "I'll be there shortly," Danny assured the officer.

Once he and Emily were alone in the reception area, Danny asked, "Do you want to go back to Eternal Rest, too? If you want to run any errands or just hide out somewhere else, I totally understand."

"I would love to hide out somewhere else, as you put it, but these are my guests. I need to be there at the house with them."

"I just need to drop this evidence off at the station first, then we'll be on our way."

As Danny drove, Emily took several photos of the tiny scrap of paper with her cell phone. She recognized the symbols from the sheet of paper in the dining room, but she wished she knew what they meant. Piper had thought the circle and triangle represented driving a wedge between people, and Serenity had said the heart with pins in it was used to figuratively pierce someone's heart, but the others didn't have any clear meaning to Emily.

Danny wasn't inside the police station for long, and Emily stared at the photos while she waited in his truck. Even though the wait couldn't have been more than ten minutes, the witches had all disappeared upstairs by the time Emily got back to Eternal Rest. Danny had stayed outside to chat with the officers on duty, and it felt odd for the house to be so silent, even though it was full of guests.

Expecting they were all resting, Emily quietly made a beeline for the kitchen, where she poured two giant glasses of sweet tea. She went onto the front porch with them, and Danny joined her on the swing after he wrapped up his conversation.

"They're in their rooms," Emily told Danny as he took a long drink.

"I guess I can wait until later to ask them about the symbols, but I have to admit, I'm anxious to know what they mean. We didn't find anything like them when we searched Helen's room yesterday."

"She didn't have them in any of her books?"

"She only had two books with her. One was about magical herbs, and the other was an almanac."

Emily looked at Danny in surprise. "Didn't she have a notebook of some kind with her own research notes and spells in it? All the other witches have one, or at least a version of it on their laptops."

"We didn't find anything like that," Danny said, frowning. "If it exists, it's not in the room she was staying in."

"She was the leader of this coven. I find it unlikely she would have come here without her own collection of knowledge. That means one of the other witches took it."

"Probably her killer."

"Not necessarily," Emily said thoughtfully. "Maybe Abbie took the book to learn more and to boost her chances of becoming the next coven leader. Perhaps they took it as a group to keep Helen's work secret from outsiders."

"We'll ask them about it. They might not want me to see what's inside, but if there's a way to decipher these symbols in there, it could help us figure out what Helen had going on."

"And why she's still drawing those symbols after her death."

Danny suddenly chuckled. "The murder cases you're involved in just get more and more strange. I fully expect alien abduction to be part of the next one!"

"Ha, ha," Emily said dryly, shaking her head.

Danny drained the last of his iced tea from his glass, then stood. "I'm going back to the station. Let's allow your guests to rest for a while. I'll deliver dinner here tonight, and maybe after a nap and some food, they'll be more willing to cooperate. I'll see you in a few hours."

"Bye, Danny." Emily stayed on the swing long after Danny had driven off, her fingers wrapped around the cold glass and her toes pushing against the wooden boards to keep her moving slowly back and forth.

Just as she was preparing to head inside, a car slowed on the road and turned into the driveway. Emily recognized Reed's car, and she came down the porch steps to meet him, too curious about the reason for his visit to wait.

Reed had opened his door but not yet climbed out of the driver's seat when Emily nearly pounced on him. "What's going on? Is everything okay?" she asked.

"Nothing is going on, and everything is just fine," Reed answered, as unflappable as ever. "I'm here to check on you, but I think I already got my answer about how you're doing."

Emily grimaced. "Sorry, I'm just a bit on edge because all this is so mysterious. You want some sweet tea while I talk?"

"I'd love some."

Soon, Emily found herself again on the swing, sipping sweet tea with a friend, but this time, it was with Reed. She described the symbols Helen had drawn while both living and dead, and she passed her phone to Reed so he could take a look at the photos of the paper that had been found on Helen's body.

Reed put his glass down on the floor so he could hold the phone with both hands. He zoomed in on some of the symbols, and now and then he muttered, "Hmm."

"Well, what do you think?" Emily asked when Reed finally handed the phone back to her.

"You said the witches interpreted these symbols as dark magic, but I disagree," Reed said, picking up his glass again. "I think I've seen one of those symbols before, and it's right next door in your cemetery."

"I didn't recognize any of the symbols," Emily said,

looking at a photo of the tiny piece of paper again. "Which one? And what headstone is it on?"

"It's that one, the one that looks like a headstone itself. See how it has those arrows all around it, pointing outward? I think that symbol is on a headstone in the southeastern area of Hilltop, though I can't remember who's buried there."

"Let's go look!" Emily jumped up from the swing.

Soon, she and Reed were inside Hilltop, each walking slowly and peering at headstones. "How could I have never noticed such an unusual engraving on one of my own headstones?" Emily asked Reed, who was standing a few yards away, bent at the waist to stare at a marker.

"Because it's on the back of the headstone, almost at ground level. Here, I found it."

Emily hurried over to Reed, who knelt and pushed the grass at the bottom of the headstone out of the way. As he had said, the symbol of a headstone surrounded by outward-facing arrows was carved near the bottom. When Reed moved his hand, the grass sprang up again and nearly obscured the symbol.

"No wonder I never saw it," Emily said, crouching down and putting her fingers against the carving. "If someone put this here, I'm guessing it's not a negative symbol, then."

"I expect it's the opposite. Helen wasn't drawing this to curse anyone, but to ward off a curse or any kind of negative energy. See how the arrows are pointed outward? It's like they're surrounding and protecting the grave."

"So does that mean Helen thought one of the other witches was trying to work dark magic against her, and she was shielding herself with this symbol? Maybe she tucked that little piece of paper inside her watchband to protect herself. If one of the witches was trying to hurt her, that could be our killer. Maybe that's why Helen's ghost drew these symbols again: to tell us to investigate that possibility."

"Maybe," Reed answered. "Or maybe she's afraid whomever was working dark magic against her when she was alive is still doing it now that she's dead. She might be worried about being made to suffer in the spirit world."

Emily shook her head. "No, if that were the case, I think she would have drawn these symbols privately, not right there in the room with all of us. She was trying to tell us something with these."

Reed grinned at Emily. "I guess it's time to go straight to the source and ask Helen's ghost what she's trying to get across with these symbols."

"She hasn't been a superb communicator yet, but I'll call Sage and ask her to give it a shot." Emily stood and stretched her arms over her head, yawning. "I think my guests had the right idea. I could use a nap, too."

"This is your chance to get some one-on-one time with Helen," Reed noted.

"Would you like to stay and help?"

Reed quickly agreed, and as they began the walk back to Eternal Rest, Emily pulled out her phone and called Sage. When Sage answered, Emily could hear how tired her best friend sounded.

"Em, you know I'd love to chat with Helen," Sage said, after Emily had laid out her thoughts. "Unfortunately, I can't. It took everything I had to make it through my appointments with clients today. I'm going straight to bed. You can do it, though. Helen even appeared to you, so she's got a connection to you already. Plus, you've got Reed there to help you."

Emily laughed. "I don't think I mentioned Reed was here."

"You didn't. I might be tired, but I'm still psychic. Good luck, Em!"

Emily was relieved when she got back to the house and realized her guests were still upstairs. She and Reed headed straight for the dining room. Reed shut the door and drew the curtains while Emily fished out a small candle she had in the sideboard. She knew it wasn't necessary, especially when it was still daylight outside, but since Sage always used a candle, it would feel strange to have a séance without one.

It felt strange enough to have a séance without Sage.

*I wish Trevor were here. I need all the help I can get.*

Emily lit the candle, turned off the lights, and sat down at the table across from Reed. She took a deep breath, closed her eyes, and said, "Helen Harper, are you here with us? We want to ask you about those symbols you drew. If you're here, can you please give us a sign?"

"The flame just flickered," Reed said quietly. "I think she's here."

Emily kept her eyes shut as she tried to sense Helen's presence. "Helen, we know that one of the symbols you drew was for protection. We found the paper you had under your watchband when you went to the cemetery the night you were killed, and it had the same symbol on it. Who are you trying to protect yourself from?"

A cold breeze touched Emily's face, and suddenly, she felt her breath catch in her throat. Sweat broke out on her forehead despite the cold. "I'm afraid," she said.

"You're safe, Emily," Reed said firmly.

"Actually, I think the fear I'm feeling is from Helen. I feel fear, but I also feel like, like... Oh! Do you hear that? The clock ticking?"

"I don't hear it. Helen is only communicating with you." Reed's voice was level, and even amid the fear Helen was channeling through her, Emily was able to appreciate his calming presence.

"It's ticking faster. Helen, what are you trying to tell

me?" The cold surrounding Emily increased, and she instinctively drew her arms around herself. She felt like someone was looming behind her, a presence standing there, too close for comfort. The fear Helen was channeling spiked as Emily felt the presence getting closer. At the same time, the ticking grew louder and faster. Suddenly, Emily's eyes snapped open, even as the ticking stopped and the feeling of the presence behind her disappeared.

"We're running out of time!" she shouted.

17

Emily's hands were shaking, and she was gasping for breath, like she had run all the way from the top of Hilltop Cemetery to Eternal Rest. Reed leaped up and hurried around the table. He sat down in the chair next to Emily's and took her hands. "Emily, look at me. You're okay."

Emily stared into Reed's eyes as she breathed slowly and deeply. She squeezed his fingers, focusing on the calm she felt emanating from him.

"Your hands are freezing," Reed noted.

"I was surrounded by cold. And I felt something standing behind me. I don't think it was Helen. I think she was trying to make me feel the way she does, or did, before she died. Like someone was coming for her."

"What was that about running out of time? Were you referring to Scott and trying to help him before the witches close the barrier tomorrow?"

Emily shook her head slowly. "No. I do feel like we're running out of time to help Scott, but the feeling I had just now wasn't mine. Helen is the one who sent that through me. That's what the sound of the ticking clock was about."

Reed released Emily's hands and sat back in his chair. "Did she feel that way before she was killed? Or does she feel that way now?"

"Now, I think. I got the impression that she feels afraid,

like she's being threatened, and if we wait too long to help her…" Emily broke off and shuddered. Helen's ghost feeling that way was too much of a reminder of what Scott was going through.

Reed rose. "I think you need a cup of hot tea. It will make you feel better."

As Reed and Emily stood in the kitchen, waiting for the kettle to boil, Emily asked, "Did you feel anything during the séance?"

"Just general impressions. I think Helen was channeling so much through you that it sort of rolled off you and drifted over to me. I felt some of that fear, but also a sense of desperation."

"Mrs. Thompson sensed Helen's shock and anger right after she was murdered, and then she appeared in my bedroom to shout that Latin phrase about the mirror reflecting the evil. That all felt like a vengeful spirit. Now, Helen seems more scared than spiteful."

Reed shrugged. "Maybe she's both."

The kettle began to whistle, so Emily poured the boiling water into her teapot. She had already added spearmint and chamomile tea. She sometimes drank the blend to help her relax before bed, and she hoped it would help soothe her after her jarring encounter with Helen.

"Let's go back to the swing," Reed suggested. "It's hot outside, but I think the fresh air and sunshine is what you need after Helen tried to turn you into an icicle."

Emily loaded the teapot and two cups onto a tray, and she and Reed went onto the front porch. They swung in silence for a long time, Emily absorbed with her thoughts, and Reed, presumably, giving her the time to process all she had experienced. Emily even poured the tea and handed Reed his cup without saying a word.

"Thanks for being here today," Emily said abruptly, after she had taken a few sips.

"You're welcome."

"Trevor once pointed out how stubborn I can be about trying to do everything myself. In this situation, though, I can feel how much I need Sage here to help guide me through all of this. She would probably be chatting up a storm with Helen by now. Or she would be, if she weren't so exhausted lately."

"Your mediumship skills are growing so quickly that, someday soon, you won't feel like you need Sage to hold your hand through a séance."

"Maybe. Still, having you here today really helped. I didn't feel so intimidated about trying to communicate with Helen. I also didn't feel as alone as I sometimes do."

"You're never alone, Emily, even if one of your friends isn't physically here with you."

As if to punctuate Reed's point, a car came into view on the road, then slowed and turned into the circular driveway. A minute later, Trevor was walking up the front porch steps. Reed nudged Emily with an elbow. "I told you so," he said as he nodded a hello to Trevor.

"Did I miss something?" Trevor asked, quirking an eyebrow at Reed.

Emily and Reed burst out laughing. After the fear and tension of the séance, and her confused thoughts afterward, it felt good for Emily to have a moment of levity. "You've missed a lot," she told Trevor. "I'm glad you're here, though."

"Trevor, you are now officially on Emily duty," Reed said. "Your task is to keep her from feeling lost and lonely." Reed's tone was teasing, but Emily knew his words were sincere. She almost protested that she didn't need looking after, then checked herself. Earlier, she had wished Trevor were there, and now he was.

Reed stood. "I'm heading home, but you know I'm

willing to come back out if you want to communicate with Helen some more."

Emily rose and gave Reed a tight hug. "Thank you," she said again.

As Reed walked to his car, Trevor leaned against a porch column and narrowed his eyes at Emily. "What did I miss, and why has Reed put me on Emily watch?"

Before she could answer, the front door banged open, and Darlene rushed out. "Emily, there you are! We've found it! We know how to help Scott cross the barrier!"

Darlene grabbed Emily's arm and began to pull her into the house. With her free hand, Emily waved at Trevor to follow along. Soon, Emily was in the parlor, seated in one of the wingback chairs and surrounded by her guests.

"We've been upstairs, looking through our books and notes," Darlene began excitedly.

"We came here to strengthen the protective barrier around Oak Hill, but as it turns out, there's also a way to remove a psychic wall," Serenity said.

"But, of course, removing the entire barrier would be dangerous," Piper added. "We can modify the spell we found so we'll just be removing a small part of it. Making a little hole in it, really."

"Right." Darlene held up her hands to form an *O* with her fingers. "That means we won't be working magic on Scott directly, but on the barrier itself. We'll use the spell we found to remove just enough of the barrier so that Scott can slip through. As soon as he's safe, we'll immediately close that spot."

"We will definitely need your friend's help, but I believe we can do it," Abbie said. Unlike the others, she didn't sound excited at the discovery. Rather, she sounded collected and confident.

Emily could only nod, feeling hope grow even while

telling herself not to get too excited. Finally, she managed to say quietly, "Thank you."

The witches began talking to each other, and Malena and Piper actually high-fived. The din was so loud Emily barely heard the doorbell ring. She began to rise, but Trevor put a hand on her shoulder. "I'll get it," he said.

A few minutes later, Trevor returned to the parlor and announced, "Dinner is served, ladies." He gestured toward the dining room even as Emily caught a whiff of fried chicken.

"Oh, good, I'm starving!" Evelyne said loudly. The other witches seemed to feel the same, because they quickly disappeared from the parlor, still chattering rapidly with each other.

Emily stayed in her chair, shutting her eyes and tipping her head back. Trevor's voice drifted from the direction of her desk. "Kelly writes that she's excited for you."

"Thanks, Kelly," Emily called.

"By the way, Trish pulled up while I was bringing dinner in. Your baked goods are in the kitchen, ready to go for breakfast tomorrow. Come on." Emily felt Trevor's hand on her shoulder. "You need to eat something, too. I still don't know what happened to you earlier today, but whatever it was, I'm sure you need to get your energy back up."

"Can I talk you into bringing me a plate? I need a little break from people right now."

Trevor quickly agreed, appearing again a few minutes later to hand Emily a plate of fried chicken, mashed potatoes, and coleslaw. As he turned away, Emily said, "Aren't you going to eat, too?"

"Of course I am. You said you need a break from people, though, so I'm going to hang out with the witches and see what other magic they're willing to teach me." With that, Trevor disappeared, leaving Emily alone.

Instead of feeling relieved about the privacy, she actually felt a little lonely. She made it through her mashed potatoes before she sighed and moved to the dining room.

Danny was aggressively biting into a chicken wing while eyeing Trevor, who was chatting with Evelyne and Piper at the other end of the table. At the same time, Abbie was talking to Danny, seemingly unaware that his attention was elsewhere. "No, like I already told you, I've never seen any of those symbols before. Perhaps Helen had devised her own power sigils," she was saying.

"At least one of them wasn't of her own design," Emily said. All the chairs were taken, so she leaned against the doorframe and stabbed at her coleslaw while she spoke. "The one that looks like a headstone surrounded by arrows is an old symbol. It's on a grave marker out in the cemetery."

Everyone fell silent, and Malena stopped eating with her fork halfway to her mouth.

"Reed showed me," Emily continued. "He thinks it's a symbol for protection."

"Emily and I were agreeing earlier that the symbols might have been in Helen's notebook. Do any of you know where that might be found?" Danny added.

Abbie frowned. "Her grimoire? It would have been in her room. Either the police took it as evidence, or we put it back in her suitcase with her other things." She looked around at the other witches. "I don't remember seeing it, though. Do any of you?"

The other five women shook their heads.

"She would have brought it here with her," Evelyne noted. "It has to be somewhere." She was looking at Abbie, her suspicion clear on her face.

"There's valuable knowledge in that grimoire," Piper said.

"Dangerous knowledge, you mean," Serenity countered, an edge in her voice.

The happy chatter after discovering how to help Scott was gone, replaced by a stony silence and accusatory glares.

"So much for my idea that a good dinner would help us get somewhere," Danny called to Emily.

Emily could only shrug before returning her attention to her dinner. Trevor had been right: after her afternoon, she was starving. She even helped herself to another heaping pile of mashed potatoes.

To Emily's relief, the witches relaxed as they continued to eat, and by the time everyone was moving on to the apple pie Danny had brought, they were again talking to each other normally.

While Emily took the take-out boxes to the trash can outside the back door, her guests moved to the tent. Only Trevor was still in the house when she returned to the parlor. "Danny went with them to keep an eye on things," he told Emily from his spot on the sofa. The corners of his lips tilted downward. "He's been really short with me tonight. Did I do something to make him angry?"

*Maybe he's jealous because you're a good-looking single guy, and you're here to help me.* Emily suspected it might be the truth, especially after the way Danny had been giving Trevor side-eye at dinner. Instead of saying that out loud, though, Emily simply shrugged and said, "Maybe he's upset that every time I get myself into a dangerous situation, you're right there with me."

"Not every time," Trevor said in a tone of mock innocence.

"Come on. Let's go see what the witches are up to."

Emily led the way to the side yard and found Danny standing just outside the tent, watching the witches closely, but there really wasn't much to see. They had drawn their chairs into a tight circle and were talking in low voices to each other. The sides of the tent had been rolled up so the evening breeze could flow through it.

"What have we missed?" Emily asked.

"They did a little reconciliation ritual," Danny said. "Abbie said it was to clear out any negative energy from their discussion about Helen's notebook. Now, they're discussing the ritual they're about to do in the cemetery." Danny finally turned his attention away from the group to focus on Emily. "Are you okay? You seem a little off tonight."

"I've been waiting for that story myself," Trevor said.

Emily took a few steps back to make sure her guests couldn't overhear her, then quickly told Trevor and Danny about her séance with Helen.

"That explains why Reed thought you needed looking after," Trevor said when she had finished.

"Why do you need looking after?" Darlene asked. While Emily had been talking, the witches had finished their discussion, and Emily hadn't noticed Darlene moving in their direction.

"My friend Reed is worried I'll get myself into trouble if I don't have adult supervision," Emily said, trying to keep her tone playful. She wasn't sure what Helen had been trying to communicate during the séance, and she wasn't quite ready to share what she had experienced with her guests. Emily was still trying to sort it all out in her mind and wondering if Helen's channeled feelings had included a valuable clue to who had killed her.

"You've got us to look after you," Darlene said in an affronted tone. "We're heading to the cemetery for our third and final energy-raising ritual. I assume you're all coming along?"

"Of course." Emily linked her arm through Darlene's

and began to walk with her. Trevor and Danny trailed behind.

Once everyone reached the top of the hill inside the cemetery, the witches again fanned out into a line like they had the previous two nights. Emily moved onto the grass behind them so she could watch, picking her way carefully between low headstones.

Emily's toe caught something, and she stumbled. Grumbling, she looked down at the spot but saw nothing. She pulled her phone out of her pocket to shine its light on the ground, chastising herself for not bringing a real flashlight. Something gold gleamed in the grass, illuminated by the glow of the phone.

It was a knife.

# 18

"Danny!" Emily called in a stage whisper. "Come here!" She kept her eyes fixed on the knife, as if it might disappear if she looked away.

When Danny rushed to Emily's side, she pointed. "Look! Do you think that's what killed Helen?"

Unlike Emily, Danny did have a flashlight, and he bent down and shined the beam on the knife. Something red glinted on the hilt. "How did we not find this in our search?" he muttered to himself.

"Because this isn't where Helen was killed," Emily noted. "There was a lot more space between them that first night, so whomever stabbed her must have stashed the knife over here."

Danny was shaking his head as he straightened up. "We made a thorough search of this cemetery. We would have noticed a gold knife sitting on the ground like this."

"Do you think it's a plant?" Emily asked, her lips barely moving.

"Yes, but let's not let your guests know I think that. Play along, and let's see what happens."

Danny pulled out his cell phone and made a call. Like Emily, his eyes never left the knife. As he spoke quietly, Emily could hear the raised voices of the witches. They seemed oblivious to what was happening behind them as they stood in a line facing west, going through the same chant they had used the previous night.

It seemed like only seconds after Danny hung up his phone that the four police officers guarding the front and back of Eternal Rest came hurrying up the hill. At Danny's silent command, they spread out behind the witches.

Emily hadn't even noticed Trevor walking up beside her, and she jumped when he said, "It looks like a witch's ceremonial dagger. It even has a ruby in the hilt."

"Since when do you know about witchcraft?" Emily nearly laughed at him.

"I've seen movies. Plus, in college, one of my graphic design professors assigned us a project where we had to pretend we were working for a client in the Middle Ages. I designed recruitment materials for a coven of witches, so I had to do some research."

This time, Emily did snicker. "I bet you never thought you'd use that knowledge in a murder investigation."

"Definitely not."

In a few minutes, the chanting began to quiet, then came to a complete stop. "The ritual is complete," Abbie announced loudly. With their work done, the witches began to turn and walk toward each other. It was Piper who noticed they had a line of police officers standing behind them, and she fell silent, staring at them.

"What is this?" Abbie asked, looking at Danny.

"This is a reminder that you are all suspects in a murder investigation, especially since we just discovered what we believe is the knife used to kill Helen Harper." Danny crossed his arms and looked at each of the witches in turn. None of them flinched under his gaze.

Abbie began to walk toward Danny, but he held up a hand as an officer stepped toward her. "Stay where you are," Danny warned. "This is once again an active crime scene, and a team is going to come collect the evidence.

Which one of you has a gold knife with a ruby in the hilt?"

Every single witch raised a hand.

"All of you?" Danny sounded surprised.

"That's what our ceremonial daggers look like," Serenity said, glancing nervously at the other women in her coven.

"Ah-ha! I was right," Trevor whispered in Emily's ear.

"Did you all bring one of these knives with you to Eternal Rest?" Danny asked.

Six heads nodded.

Danny turned his attention to the four police officers. "We're going to escort these ladies to the tent. They will wait there while we search their rooms to see whose knife is missing."

"Oh, come on!" Piper said, throwing her hands up. "We're exhausted. We did a death ritual for Helen and an energy-raising ritual today. Our coven leader is dead, we're practically at each other's throats because we don't know who did it, and we all just want to go to bed."

"Too bad," Danny answered tersely. "Remember, the sooner we find Helen's killer, the sooner you can all go home and sleep as much as you want."

The witches grumbled all the way down the hill, and Emily couldn't blame them. She expected Danny was purposely being short with them, but she didn't know why.

Once the witches were seated in the tent, surrounded by the four police officers, Danny said to Emily, "I'll need keys to each guest room."

"Of course. I'll get them from my desk, then get something for my guests to drink."

"I'll serve the drinks for you, Emily," Trevor said. As Emily was thanking him, she heard a noise behind her and turned to see three more police cars pulling to a stop in front of the house.

*The whole town will be talking about this over breakfast tomorrow.*

"Ladies, before we do our search, is there anything you would like to say?" Danny said to the women.

The witches remained stoically silent, and Emily could sense the rising tension between them. Between the earlier strife about the whereabouts of Helen's notebook and the discovery of the knife, they were only becoming more suspicious of each other. The folding chairs, which had been so close together before, were now spread out under the large tent.

Emily led Danny into the house, retrieved her ring of keys, and handed them over. "If one of their knives is missing, they're being framed. That's your speculation, right?" Emily glanced upward, picturing the guest rooms on the second floor.

"Right. If we can find out who's being framed, that means our killer had something against both Helen and the person whose knife is missing. This could help us narrow in on who's guilty."

"Too bad we can't just make them cast a truth-telling spell," Emily said, shaking her head.

"That's a great idea. If magic is real, then a truth-telling spell would save me a lot of work."

"Unfortunately, I don't have one handy."

"Me, neither. At the moment, I just want them to believe we've found the actual murder weapon. I was purposely treating them rudely, and we're going to take our time with the search. A nap and dinner didn't help me get anywhere with information earlier, so maybe the opposite will work: get them tired, angry, and ready to point fingers at each other. In fact, I might tell Trevor to skip the drinks."

Emily shook her head firmly. "No. They're my guests,

Danny. I'm going to treat them with respect, and I expect you to do the same."

"With that attitude, they might be your guests for longer than you planned. It will be faster if we can wear them down."

Emily's jaw tightened. "They're my guests," she repeated, enunciating each word.

Danny sighed, and his shoulders slumped slightly. "All right. I'll tell my team to make the search as quickly as they can."

Emily returned to the tent slowly. She wasn't upset with Danny, and she could understand his logic that making her guests uncomfortable might get them to open up, but she doubted staying up late and not having a drink would be enough to get a murder confession from anyone. Still, she didn't like the idea that he wanted her guests to be anything but comfortable and cared for at Eternal Rest. Or, she told herself, as comfortable and cared for as they could possibly be when they were all essentially under house arrest.

Emily gazed around the tent, wondering if her guests felt as frustrated as she did.

Serenity was actually sitting on the grass, her legs crossed and her hands resting palms upward. Her eyes were closed, and she was softly chanting words Emily couldn't hear well enough to understand.

Piper was pacing back and forth, her hands tapping against the legs of her navy-blue slacks as she grumbled angrily.

Abbie sat regally in her chair, her spine straight and a look on her face that was both defiant and confident. Emily noted with a little envy that the more pressure Abbie was under, the more beautiful she looked.

Malena sat with her legs stretched out in front of her, her arms crossed as she glared at the house impatiently.

Darlene and Evelyne, at least, were talking to each other, and Emily was relieved to see not all of her guests were giving each other the silent treatment.

Emily sank down in a chair and leaned forward until her head was resting on her knees. With one hand, she reached back and pulled her low ponytail loose so that her hair fell down like a curtain around her face. She was feeling too many emotions to count. Between having a murder investigation happening at her own house and feeling anxious about helping Scott's spirit get through the barrier in time, Emily felt overwhelmed and exhausted.

It wasn't until Emily felt a gentle hand on her back that she finally sat up, pushing her hair behind her ears. Trevor was standing there with a cup of coffee, which Emily gratefully accepted.

Trevor carried a chair over to Emily and sat down next to her, his own cup of coffee steaming away in his hand. "If it's a plant," he said under his breath, "then how did one of them get into someone else's room to steal their knife?"

"Danny would be happy to let them sit out here and starve until they tell him that," Emily said darkly.

"Really?"

"No." Emily blew on her coffee, then took a tentative sip. It was still too hot to drink. "But he is hoping they might give up some info if they're worn out enough."

"I don't know that anyone but the killer has much left to tell," Trevor said, glancing toward the witches. "I think they're scared, and I don't know that you and I can appreciate how they're feeling right now. Their coven is like a family, a sisterhood, and they know one of their sisters killed another one. It must be terrifying."

"I can't completely relate, but don't forget, one of the suspects is my own mother-in-law."

"But you're certain it wasn't her."

"I can't even consider her as a suspect. Not Darlene."

"Then that only leaves five possibilities. Who do we start with?"

"What, are you going to interrogate my guests?"

"No, I thought—" Trevor was cut off by a muffled scream.

"It's her! I just saw her!" Serenity was clutching her face with both hands, staring toward Eternal Rest. "In the window!"

Emily whipped her head around but saw no one in the windows along the side of the house. "Who, Serenity? Where?"

"Helen! She was right there!" Serenity pointed toward the parlor window.

"Stop it, Serenity," Abbie snapped. "You're making that up."

"Why would I make it up? She was staring out the window, and her lips were moving. She's still trying to work magic against us!" Serenity drew her knees up and wrapped her arms around them. "She doesn't know who killed her, so she's going to hurt all of us!"

"Shut your mouth!" Abbie stood, her face contorted with anger. "You're only saying that to scare everyone!"

"I saw her, too," Piper said, her voice barely audible. She had stopped her pacing and was staring toward the same window Serenity had indicated. "I don't think she's working magic against us, though. I think Helen is trying to help us."

19

"What makes you say that?" Malena stood and moved so she was right next to Piper. She leaned forward slightly as she squinted at the window.

Instead of answering Malena, Piper asked, "Did you see her face, Serenity? You were right that her lips were moving, but she looked worried."

Emily instantly thought of the form she had felt looming behind her during the séance. "I think she feels threatened, even though she's already dead. Reed and I communicated with Helen earlier, and she channeled a feeling of something standing just behind her. It was a creepy feeling, a scary one."

Darlene's head swiveled toward Emily. "You didn't tell us you'd gotten more information from her."

Emily shrugged. "I guess I wasn't ready to talk about it." Earlier, Emily had thought she didn't want to tell her guests about the séance because she was still trying to figure out how Helen's communication was tied to the case. At the moment, though, Emily was struck with the sudden thought that by admitting she was communicating with Helen's ghost, she might be making herself the next target.

*I'll be locking my bedroom door tonight and sleeping with one eye open.*

"If you're able to communicate with Helen, then we

don't need to wait for your friend," Abbie said, rising in one fluid motion. "Let's go ask Helen if she's trying to hurt us or help us."

Abbie began to move toward the house, and the other witches hurried to join her.

"Whoa!" Emily called, holding out her hands. "Don't forget, the house is off limits while the police are searching it. We have to wait."

"We do, but you don't," Evelyne pointed out. "You can go talk to her right now. Let us know what she says."

Emily's guests, standing together as one group now, stared at her expectantly, and she felt nervous at the idea of not only trying to communicate with Helen again, but also at the idea of trying to appease the witches.

"I'll go with you," Trevor said quietly. With words of encouragement following them, Trevor and Emily left the tent and walked slowly toward the house.

"I don't know that I can do this," Emily told Trevor. "I'm exhausted, and I'm a little scared."

"Even if you can't," Trevor said, a lopsided smile on his face, "it gives us a break from all of them for a while."

In the parlor, the first thing Emily noticed was handwriting on the paper by her laptop. The pen next to it was still rolling slowly to a stop. Kelly's big, swooping handwriting read simply, *She's too tired now.*

"Thanks for letting me know, Kelly." Emily picked up the paper and put a fresh sheet in its place. "I guess I'm not the only one who's too worn out to communicate. I'll let our guests know that we'll try again tomorrow."

Before Emily and Trevor reached the front door on their way back to the tent, Danny's voice sounded from upstairs. "Emily, wait for me. We're finished with the search."

Emily turned, feeling her trepidation growing even as she asked, "And?"

"All six of your guests have a shiny gold knife among their belongings. However, when we searched Helen's room on Friday, we did not find a knife."

"The one we found tonight was Helen's, then."

Danny nodded grimly. "I had thought the knife was a plant to make one of the women look guilty, but I think we have to consider this really was the murder weapon."

"If that's true, then how did the police miss it in the initial search?" Emily was frowning. She knew how thorough the Oak Hill Police Department was in their work, and it didn't make sense that they had simply overlooked something she had quite literally tripped over.

Danny shook his head. "I don't know. We also have to learn whether Helen took the knife with her that night, and her killer seized the opportunity to use it on her, or if her killer stole it from her room prior to leaving for the cemetery."

"Which would mean it was a pre-meditated murder," Trevor said.

"Yes," Danny agreed grudgingly. Again, Emily caught the quick but sharp look Danny threw at Trevor.

*Does he think they're competing for me?*

"Oh, no." The words escaped Emily's mouth before she could stop herself, and both men looked at her expectantly. "Nothing," she stammered awkwardly. "I was just thinking over all the information."

*Well, it's not a lie.*

"I think it's time for us all to get some sleep. It's been a long day." Danny put a hand on Emily's arm. "Will you be okay? Do you want me to stay here to keep an eye on things?"

Emily wasn't sure if Danny was offering as a detective, as a friend, or as a romantic hopeful, but she couldn't bring herself to look into his brown eyes as she answered, "I'll be fine. We have the four officers guarding the house."

The police who had been assisting in the search began to file down the stairs, and Emily quickly moved to make room for them. As Danny followed them outside, Trevor hung back and asked Emily, "Do you want me to stay?"

"Thanks, but your Emily duty is finished for today. I appreciate you coming over, though."

"Call me if you need anything." Trevor gave Emily a quick, reassuring squeeze on the shoulder, and a moment later, she was standing alone in the parlor, feeling slightly flustered. But her thoughts, at least, weren't on murder for the moment.

On Sunday morning, Emily was halfway to the dining room with the breakfast trays before she realized she had forgotten both the cheese and the jam. With a low groan, she turned and headed back to the kitchen. She had slept very little the night before, worried she might be the killer's next target, worried that Danny's promise to back off on the romantic gestures had been short-lived, and—more than anything—worried something would go wrong with the spell to bring Scott through the barrier that night.

With so much on her mind, Emily was frankly surprised she had remembered to put breakfast out at all.

Once the cheese and jam had been added to the meats, Grainy Day baked goods, and butter, Emily swept up the trays and returned to the dining room. It wasn't until she had put them down on the sideboard that she noticed the piece of paper there was again covered in writing.

It appeared that, overnight, both Kelly and Helen had been trying to communicate. Kelly's writing was difficult to read, many of the letters obscured by the same symbols Helen had once again scrawled all over the paper. It didn't help that Kelly had written in the small, timid letters she used when she was scared. *The anger is growing again. Fear still, but so much anger.*

Was Helen back in vengeful spirit mode? "I guess Reed was right," Emily murmured to herself. "Helen is both vengeful and scared. Vengeful I get, but why scared? What's happening to her in the spirit world?"

Emily told Kelly to keep up the good work, then returned to the kitchen for her third cup of coffee.

By the time the witches came downstairs for breakfast, Emily was at her desk in the parlor, scrolling through her emails without really absorbing anything in them. She had tried to confirm a reservation request that had been submitted through the Eternal Rest website, but she was feeling so groggy she decided to do it later, when she was less likely to make a mistake.

The sound of raised voices snapped Emily into wake-fulness.

"How can you say that?" Serenity sounded angry and hurt.

"Because it's true!" Abbie's voice was just as loud, but it sounded as though she were keeping her emotions in better check than Serenity. "No wonder you recognized those symbols she drew! You claim to be into all this love and positivity magic, but you were working against Helen to get rid of her as coven leader."

"Not by using dark magic! I was doing spells to make her see her errors. She needed to realize she was leading this coven down a dangerous path. I used that symbol to pierce her heart with the truth! I never did anything to hurt her!"

Someone else spoke quietly—Emily thought it might be Evelyne—before Abbie said in an icy tone, "Don't defend her. You wanted the position back, so I'm sure you were helping Serenity bring Helen down. I dreamed of you last night. You were standing in front of me, and my back was up against a wall. I don't know if you two are already working magic against me, or if it's a sign of things to come."

"You're making the assumption you'll be our next coven leader, Abbie," Malena pointed out. Rather than sounding upset, like the others, she simply sounded bored, like she was tired of all the drama.

Emily sat back in her desk chair, too absorbed in eavesdropping to do anything else. She had left the paper there on the sideboard, and she was sure the witches must have discovered it. Maybe that was what had prompted this latest argument.

"Mrs. Thompson, are you there?" Emily called. When a quiet knock sounded on the wall, Emily continued. "I'm sure Helen was very angry when she realized she had been murdered. Now, Kelly says she feels anger again. I had assumed it was coming from Helen, but I'm thinking maybe Kelly is feeling anger from one of our living guests. Am I correct in that guess?"

One knock confirmed Emily's assumption. Helen wasn't being a vengeful spirit at all. At least, not at the moment. One of the other witches was so angry, their emotion was having an impact on Kelly and Mrs. Thompson.

Or, judging by the raised voices still coming from the dining room, more than one of Emily's guests was radiating anger.

Emily knew that for the rest of her life, her idea of a bad guest would be defined by the arrogant, ungrateful Jaxon Knight-MacGinn. At the moment, though, as she sat there listening to the squabbling of her guests, she actually found herself thinking she would rather be dealing with him.

*Tonight we help Scott, and then the witches will strengthen the barrier. Hopefully, we identify the murderer, too, so they can all go home, and I can have some peace.*

"Emily?"

Emily turned and saw Malena standing there, her fingers twisting together nervously. She had closed the parlor door behind her. "Malena, are you okay?"

"No." Malena began to walk toward the sofa, but halfway there, she abruptly changed direction and moved toward the side window. As Emily watched, Malena made a full circle around the room, still wringing her hands as she breathed in and out loudly. "I need to talk to the detective, but I'm scared. I thought I would tell you first, so you can help me tell him."

"Tell him what, Malena?" Emily half rose from her chair.

"That I'm the one who took Helen's knife. I'm the one who left it out there in the cemetery."

*I'm trapped in my parlor with a killer.*

Emily wondered if she should act casually or try to fight her way to the door so she could flee. She stood, frozen in indecision, as Malena stopped her pacing and faced Emily. "I just wanted something to remember her by!" she cried. Malena balled her hands into fists and pressed them against her mouth.

"Okay," Emily said gently, taking a tentative step toward Malena. "What do you mean you wanted something to remember her by?"

Malena sniffed loudly. "Her ceremonial dagger. I took it. Helen's room was unlocked—she was notorious for losing keys, so she didn't lock the door to her room when we went out for the ritual the night she… Anyway, after we all went to bed that night, I snuck into her room and took her dagger. I wanted a memento of Helen. It wasn't until the next day, when the police really started grilling us, that I learned she'd been stabbed. I realized if I was found with her dagger, it might make me look bad. Like maybe I had used it to—you know. I couldn't run out and hide it, since the police are watching us so closely. So, I took it with me when I went and found you in the cemetery yesterday, and I threw it as far as I could when the officer following me wasn't looking."

When Malena was finished talking, she seemed to shrink into herself, her head and shoulders drooping and her arms pulled in tight against her body. Emily simply stared at her for a long while, too shocked to say anything. Malena hadn't just confessed to stealing Helen's knife. She had also shared the information that Helen's room had been unlocked, meaning anyone could have gone in there to remove evidence or take her notebook. It would have been so easy to get up in the middle of the night and sneak in there, and no one would have been the wiser.

Emily wasn't sure if she was trying to calm herself or Malena when she said, "I'm sure Danny will understand. I'll call him right now and ask him to come out. It's going to be okay, Malena."

Emily retreated into her bedroom to call Danny. She didn't try to relay any part of Malena's story. Instead, she simply told him in a quavering tone that he needed to come immediately to take a statement.

Fifteen minutes later, Emily opened the front door to let Danny inside the house. He put his hands on her shoulders and said, "You're so pale. You've had a big shock."

"Malena is in the parlor waiting for you. I'll be in the kitchen." Emily was still too absorbed in thought to say anything more than that. If the gold knife she had stumbled across in the cemetery hadn't been used to kill Helen, after all, then where was the actual murder weapon? Did one of her guests still have it stashed away in their room, hidden so well even the police hadn't been able to find it? Was it still out in the cemetery somewhere?

Emily sat at the kitchen table, a cup of coffee sitting untouched in front of her, as she went through all the possibilities again and again in her mind. Eventually, Danny joined her, sitting down heavily in the other chair. "Well," he said.

Emily sighed. "We're back to not having the murder

weapon, and we have to consider the fact that if Helen's room was unlocked, anyone could have taken anything from it."

"Which means someone probably did sneak in there and take her notebook," Danny said, nodding. "We didn't find it during our search of the rooms, but whomever took it might have had it with them at the time. Did they take it as a souvenir, like Malena taking the knife, or did they take it because they thought it might hold some incriminating information?"

Emily didn't bother to answer Danny, since he knew as well as she did that neither of them knew the truth of Helen's missing notebook. She simply sat and stared down into her coffee cup, lost in thought again. Vaguely, as if he were far away, Emily heard Danny get up, followed by the clink of a coffee cup being set on the countertop. He sat down again a moment later, just as a thought struck Emily.

"Malena didn't know Helen had been stabbed until the police told her," she said.

"That's what she told me, as well. That news is what prompted her to get rid of the knife."

"Right. But don't you think it's strange that she didn't already know? Evelyne said she was the one who took a look at Helen, and she knew right away CPR was pointless. She said she had been a nurse."

"You saw how Helen was positioned," Danny said. "From the right angle, even the blood on her shirt wouldn't have been visible since she was on her side."

"Evelyne must have realized how Helen had died, though," Emily insisted. "Wouldn't she have shared that information with her own coven?"

"She might not have realized. Yes, she had been a nurse, but out there, in the dark, scared and upset, she probably couldn't tell the cause of death right away."

"Hmm," Emily said, not convinced by Danny's logic.

"Do you think Evelyne might have killed Helen herself, then only pretended to try to help her?"

"Helen was the one who got Evelyne kicked out as coven leader," Emily reminded Danny. "But, you're right, it's a far-fetched theory. The problem is that every idea I come up with seems far-fetched."

"Then," Danny said, leaning across the table and raising his eyebrows, "it's a good thing you're not the detective assigned to the case."

"Thank goodness!"

"You're also not the psychic assigned to the case." The voice came from the kitchen doorway, and Emily looked up to see Sage standing there in a pair of gray sweatpants and a black T-shirt that read *I Need Coffee* on it. She was clutching a pillow in one arm.

"Are you going to a sleepover?" Emily was amused, but she was also worried Sage's lackluster ensemble was a sign of her worsening exhaustion.

"No, but I'm planning to nap while I'm here today. I want to conserve as much energy as possible for our ritual with Scott tonight. First, though, I want to have a talk with Helen Harper."

Danny stood. "I'd love to stay and watch you in action, but I need to get back to the station. Ladies, let me know if you need anything." Danny was speaking to both of them, but his eyes were fixed on Emily.

By the time Emily returned to the kitchen after escorting Danny to the front door, Sage had already poured her own cup of coffee and was sitting at the table. "Something is off here," she said calmly.

"Probably because I have a scared, angry ghost and a murderer in my house," Emily said, sinking down into her chair again.

"No, it's not either of those things. What I'm feeling is"

—Sage spread her hands, her fingers waggling—"like an illusion. A deception."

Emily lowered her voice. "These witches are all out to get each other. Serenity has been shouting at Abbie this morning."

"The truth behind the sweet exterior," Sage said. "That's exactly the sort of vibe I'm sensing, but I don't think it's coming from Serenity. I passed her on my way down the hall, and even though I could feel frustration radiating off her, I could also feel her sorrow. I think Helen's murder and all this discord is heartbreaking for her."

"Maybe Helen can point out the deception, then," Emily said, rising.

Sage held up one finger as she brought the coffee cup toward her lips. "You saw my shirt. I need coffee before I communicate."

Darlene and Serenity were the only ones in the dining room when Emily and Sage went in. Emily apologetically told them they needed the room, and Serenity's eyes widened at the mention of a séance. "Can we stay to participate?" she asked eagerly.

"Actually, we would prefer—" Emily began.

"That's a great idea," Sage cut in. Emily gave her a sideways glance, and Sage said quietly, "More energy will help both me and Helen. Besides, like I said, I think Serenity is safe. Darlene, too, of course."

*If Sage's instinct can be trusted—which it usually can—that means we're down to just four suspects, then. Piper, Evelyne, Malena, and Abbie. That's progress, I suppose.*

Sage hadn't bothered to bring her bag of séance instruments, saying Helen seemed beyond the basics of blowing out a candle or ringing a bell. She sat down and began to explain her process to Darlene and Serenity while Emily closed the door, drew the curtains, and turned off the lights. As Emily sat down, Sage was saying sternly, "I want to stress that what we experience in this room is not to be shared with anyone, not even the members of your own coven. You're now assisting in the investigation."

Serenity looked like she was going to protest having to keep secrets from her fellow witches, but Darlene nodded grimly and said, "We're ready."

"Good." Sage closed her eyes, and when she spoke again, her voice had dropped to the lower register she used when speaking with ghosts. "Helen Harper, I already know you're here with us. I can feel you. Are you ready to answer some questions for us?"

Darlene was looking around the room, clearly hoping to catch a glimpse of Helen's ghost. Serenity was biting her lip in concentration, her eyes squeezed tightly shut.

"Helen, we can't help you if you don't help us," Sage said. In her usual voice, she added, "She's here, and she hears me. I know it. For some reason, though, she isn't talking."

There was a tapping noise on the floor behind Emily, and she turned in her chair to see a pen lying at the base of the sideboard. Emily rose and looked at the paper there. *Too upset to talk,* Kelly had written.

"Kelly," Emily called, "can you tell us whom Helen is angry with?" She picked up the pen and replaced it in its normal spot, then sat down again, her back to the sideboard so Kelly could write without her looking. Sage, Serenity, and Darlene turned away, too, once Emily explained Kelly wouldn't write if she had an audience. After a few moments, Emily got up again and looked at the paper. *Upset. Not angry.*

"What is Helen upset about?" Emily asked.

Sage suddenly exhaled quickly and loudly. "Ow!"

"Are you okay?" Darlene asked, half rising from her chair.

"I feel like I've been punched in the stomach. Helen feels threatened. I sense danger, and... Oh, hang on!" Sage had opened her eyes again, and they took on an unfocused look as she gazed straight ahead. Her breathing slowed, and Emily knew Helen was channeling something through Sage.

Serenity looked from Sage to Emily with a worried expression, and Emily made a calming gesture. "It's okay," she mouthed.

"You're getting better at this, Helen," Sage said in a nearly monotone voice. "Keep going. Your sister witches are here to lend their energy to you."

Serenity looked even more worried at that, but Darlene continued to sit calmly, giving the impression she attended séances all the time. She seemed right at home watching a psychic medium at work.

After several minutes, Sage blinked her eyes rapidly a few times and sat back, finally turning her head to look at the others seated around the table. "She's channeling the idea of order being disrupted. Like a hierarchy or pecking order, it seemed. She feels like it's being threatened, and she's scared about what will happen next. Helen distinctly told me, 'It's coming, and you have to stop it.'"

"What's coming?" Darlene asked at the same time Emily said, "Stop what?"

"Abbie," Serenity whispered. She leaned forward and put her face in her hands. "We all know Helen wanted her to be the next coven leader. I've been accusing her of killing Helen, but what if she's the next one on the list? If this is about hierarchy, Abbie is at the top now. Helen might be upset because she's worried Abbie will be killed next!"

# 21

Instead of responding to Serenity's pronouncement that Abbie was going to be murdered next, Emily looked at Sage inquisitively and asked, "Does that feel right to you?"

"Does it feel right to *you*?" Sage countered.

Emily took a deep breath and closed her eyes, focusing on the room around her. She knew Sage, Darlene, and Serenity were staring at her, but she tried to push the discomfort of their gazes aside. Slowly, Emily began to feel the same fear Sage had mentioned. It was similar to what she had felt when she had tried to communicate with Helen in the parlor. Thinking of what Sage had said about a pecking order, she focused her thoughts on that, making it more of a silent question for Helen.

Briefly, so quickly she wondered if it had really happened at all, Emily saw an image flash in her mind. "Oh!" The second the word was out of her mouth, the feeling of fear disappeared. She had accidentally broken the connection she had established with Helen.

"What did you experience?" Sage asked.

"I think Helen channeled an image through me. But it was there and gone so quickly! Maybe it was just my imagination." Emily's initial excitement was already turning to doubt, and she shook her head.

"Tell us what you saw," Sage prompted. Unlike Emily,

Sage still looked excited, a little smile playing at the corners of her mouth.

"I saw a group of people, all huddled together in a tight circle." Emily paused as she tried to remember as much detail as possible. "The people were facing outward, and their arms were raised, like they were trying to ward off something."

"They were doing magic. A protection spell, maybe," Serenity suggested.

"There was something coming. I don't know what; I couldn't see it." Emily shivered. "I could sense it, though."

Sage was grinning. "Great job, Em! You just had your first channeled vision from a ghost!"

"I don't think it was good news Helen was sharing," Emily said.

"Well, no," Sage said, sobering. "But we already know she's afraid of something, so that's no surprise. I don't feel guilty about stopping to celebrate this huge achievement for you."

"Sage is right," Darlene said. She looked at Emily proudly. "Your growth means you'll be better able to help Scott tonight, when the time comes."

Emily nodded. "In the meantime, how does this vision tie in with the things Helen has already communicated?"

"I think Helen's message to me about a threat to the hierarchy didn't apply to one person within the coven," Sage said. "I think Helen might sense a threat to the coven as a whole. Their power is what's at stake."

"Or our lives," Serenity said in a shaky voice.

"But what could pose such a threat?" Emily rose and turned on the lights, then moved to the windows and threw open the curtains. She wanted as much light and sunshine as she could get to battle the rising feeling of dread she felt inside her.

Serenity's voice was stronger as she said, "This theory

could explain some of the symbols Helen has been drawing, like the heart and triangle that represent a wedge being driven between us. Maybe she wasn't trying to curse anyone at all, but trying to communicate that there's a threat to our coven, something that could break us apart."

"And the headstone surrounded by arrows was a protection symbol for the entire coven, not just for Helen," Emily suggested. "My ghosts sensed her anger, especially right after her murder. That and the Latin phrase she spoke were both about her wanting to find her killer. However, I think the fear we've been sensing from Helen is about something entirely unrelated to her murder. It's some outside threat she was worried about, even before she was killed."

"And it's something she still feels threatened by, despite being dead already," Darlene said. "Even as a ghost, she feels vulnerable."

"Which means it's likely a supernatural force she was worried about." Emily splayed her palms flat against the table, bracing herself. "Sage, you and I have both been outside the barrier. There's only one thing both of us have sensed that's dangerous enough to worry a ghost."

"You think Helen sensed the entity that's keeping Scott from coming through." Sage reached out and put a hand over one of Emily's. "Even you saw the entity a few days ago, despite the barrier. If Helen was at all psychically sensitive, she probably felt it while she was alive. Now that she's dead, I'm certain she can sense it, since the ghosts of Eternal Rest can, too."

"Why didn't I figure it out sooner? Helen channeled cold and silence through me, and both of those are clear signs the dark entity is present. She was trying to warn me."

"I'll take the blame for not seeing the connection sooner," Sage said. "You suggested you had communicated with the entity directly, and I told you that you were just in a trance while talking to Helen. I didn't even stop to consider that Helen was sending you a message about the entity."

Emily shrugged. "Neither did I. Those symbols she drew were warnings that it's coming for us—not just the coven, but all of us—and she added the protection symbol in an effort to keep us safe. That explains why Helen channeled a sense of urgency, like she was running out of time. The entity is already able to send its cold and even its consciousness through the barrier—you said you dreamed about it, Sage—and if the barrier isn't strengthened soon…"

"Then it's a good thing we're doing it tonight," Darlene said. "Even if we fail to get Scott's spirit through, we absolutely must restore the barrier's power. None of us knows what this thing is, but I do know we don't want it terrorizing Oak Hill."

Emily sighed. She wanted to argue, but she also knew Darlene was right. Scott was just one person, and a ghost, at that. Putting everyone in town in danger for the sake of one soul didn't seem worth it.

"Then we can't fail to help Scott or restore the barrier," Serenity said. She still sounded scared, but her expression was determined. "We're going to have to be united in this, Darlene. I'm worried all of our fighting is going to weaken our magic."

"If we could find out who killed Helen, it would go a long way toward healing the rift between us," Darlene said resolutely. "I'm glad we're finally figuring out what Helen has been trying to tell us, but unfortunately, none of it is giving us clues to who killed her."

"And I'm too exhausted to ask her about that," Sage said. "Em, would you like to try?"

Emily began to reply when the doorbell rang, followed by loud knocking on the door. As she rose from her chair, the doorbell rang again, and then she heard shouting. Thinking it must be Danny and that something was wrong, Emily sprinted to the door and threw it open.

She had never seen the man standing there in her life. He was of average height, his khaki pants and light-blue Oxford shirt making him look like he should be at an office rather than at the front door of Eternal Rest. His tanned face, Emily thought, was probably handsome when it wasn't twisted in rage. "Where is my wife?" the man shouted at Emily.

Emily jerked backward in surprise as the man continued to shout. "You can't keep her here! She needs to come home!"

When Emily took a step backward to put some space between her and the angry stranger, he took a step forward, crossing the threshold. At the same time, Emily saw two police officers rushing up the stairs, and she realized one of them was Roger. Each of them grabbed one of the man's arms to stop him from coming farther into the house.

"Sorry, Miss Emily," Roger said. "He told us he was expected, and there's not a rule against visitors, so we let him through."

"It's okay," Emily said, her eyes still glued to the man's face. "Maybe he'll promise to calm down, so you can let him go."

"Calm down? How could I possibly be calm right now? You can't hold my wife against her will!" The man's face was a deep shade of red, and Emily wrinkled her nose in disgust at the spittle flying from his lips. She made a mental note to mop the hallway later.

"You're Piper's husband, I assume?" Emily made the guess based solely on his clothing, which was so similar to Piper's own style.

"Yes. And unless there is evidence against her and she's under arrest, then you can't hold her."

"I'm not holding anyone," Emily said, struggling to maintain her composure. "The Oak Hill Police Department has ordered everyone to stay here until we find out who killed Helen Harper. I believe you used to date her daughter?" Emily instantly regretted asking the question, because the man's lips drew back, his teeth bared.

"That has nothing to do with anything."

Emily turned her attention to the police officers again. "Could you please escort this gentleman to the tent? I'm sure he'll find his wife there, and she can tell him that she's not going anywhere just yet."

"I can walk by myself." The man's voice was slightly quieter, though his eyes still flashed angrily. The police officers loosened their grip on his arms, and he turned and stalked off the porch.

"Great," Emily mumbled to herself as the officers followed him closely. "Just what I need: another guest, and more anger to upset my ghosts."

Emily had just pulled out her phone to call Danny and tell him he should probably head over as soon as possible when Piper's husband came rushing toward the house again. "She's not in the tent. Where is Piper?" He was shouting again, and Emily hastily put her phone back into her pocket so she could hold up both hands defensively.

"Owen, what do you think you're doing? You're making a fool of yourself." Darlene was standing in the doorway between the dining room and the hallway, and she was frowning at Owen with disapproval.

"Darlene, you can't possibly be okay with this!" Emily noticed Owen's voice was much more respectful when he spoke to Darlene.

"No, I'm not okay with this. Someone in our coven murdered Helen. One of the women who you know, possibly even your own wife, killed Helen. It is absolutely not okay."

"Piper didn't kill anyone."

"Do you know that for sure?" Darlene challenged. "She and Helen had a rocky relationship."

One corner of Owen's mouth twitched, and for a brief moment, Emily saw the fear below the anger.

*He doesn't know for sure that Piper is innocent, and he's terrified.*

"I just want to take her home."

"Then help us," Serenity said, peering around Darlene's arm. "Talk to Piper and see if you can find out whether or not she killed Helen."

"That's ridiculous," Owen spat. "You've always been ridiculous, but you want me to play detective with my own wife?" Owen rubbed the back of his neck, ruffling his neatly styled auburn hair in the process. In a quieter voice, he said, "I don't even know where she is."

"If she's not in the tent, then she must be upstairs," Emily said. "You're welcome to wait in the parlor while I go knock on her door."

"I'm coming with you," Owen said firmly.

With a sigh, Emily turned and led the way upstairs, worried Owen would start shouting again at any minute. Emily knocked on Piper's door, but there was no answer.

On the off chance Piper was in someone else's room, she knocked on those doors, too, but with no luck.

"You're sure she wasn't out there at the tent?" Emily asked Owen.

"I'm sure."

"Wait here." Emily ran downstairs and retrieved her guest room keys, then came back up and unlocked the door to Piper's room. It was empty.

"Oh, no," Emily said. "I think Piper has snuck out of the house. Again."

Emily already had her cell phone to her ear, listening to it ring, as she ran up to Roger and the other police officer. Danny answered right as she reached them, so she addressed both him and the officers at the same time. "Piper isn't in her room, and she's not out here in the tent. Did someone escort her to the cemetery again?" Emily knew the answer was no, because if she had gone there with permission, the police would have known.

"I'll be right there!" Danny said as Roger pulled out a radio, telling the two officers guarding the backside of the house to come to the tent immediately.

"She said she was going inside to get a snack," Evelyne said. "Not ten minutes ago."

"That's about the time I texted her to tell her I was almost here," Owen said. There was no anger to mask his fear now.

"I did see her go in the house," Roger said.

"And no one came out the back door," added an officer who was just hurrying into the tent.

"She could have snuck out a side window, maybe," Evelyne suggested.

"No," Emily said. "We were in the dining room, so she couldn't have gotten out that way, and the only windows in the kitchen face the back of the house, where officers were stationed. If she had crawled out a window from the parlor or my bedroom on this side of the house, everyone in the tent would have seen her."

"And if she was making a snack, she would have heard Owen shouting like a madman, and she would have come out of the kitchen," Darlene said.

"Maybe she did hear Owen, and that's exactly why we can't find her," Emily suggested. "I bet she's hiding in the house, and I think I know where."

Emily didn't bother to check the kitchen. Instead, she went straight to her bedroom, certain Piper was there. Ordinarily, Emily would lock her bedroom door when she had guests, but since she had been confined to the house so much the past few days, locking it had seemed pointless.

The bedroom was empty, but the bathroom door was shut.

*I didn't leave it like that.*

Emily crossed the room and knocked on the bathroom door. "Piper, come out."

There was no answer, except the sound of the toilet flushing, followed by a ripping sound.

Emily threw open the door and saw Piper sitting on the floor, her legs folded under her. In one hand, she held an open book. In her other, she held a page covered in handwriting. Piper looked at Emily wildly, then crumpled the page and threw it into the toilet. As she reached for the handle to flush it down, Emily's hand darted out and caught her wrist.

"Please, Emily, please!" Piper's eyes were red and swollen.

Emily felt a stab of pain for Piper and had to remind herself the woman appeared to be destroying evidence. There was no doubt in Emily's mind the book was Helen's, full of her spells and notes about her magic and her coven.

164

Piper dropped the book as Roger gently pushed his way past Emily and pulled Piper to her feet. In short order, Piper was in handcuffs.

"I didn't kill her!" Piper cried.

"You're tampering with evidence. That's cause enough for arrest." Roger looked at Piper grimly, then nudged her toward the door.

"Wait," Emily said. "Please. Piper, why do you have Helen's notebook? And why are you trying to destroy it?"

Piper glanced into Emily's bedroom, where Owen was standing perfectly still, his mouth open in shock. "I took the notebook because I wanted to prove Helen had been working dark magic against me. The problem is, I did prove it! She has spells in there designed to destroy bonds and break up relationships. I realized that if anyone else saw those spells, they would think I had killed Helen because of them."

Piper took in a big gulp of air, then tilted her head to wipe her face against her shoulder. "Plus, Owen and I nearly got divorced five years ago because we started fighting so much. I knew that if he found out about Helen's magic against us, he would be mad at me."

"Piper," Owen said, his voice surprisingly gentle. "Helen is the one I've held a grudge against all these years, and that has nothing to do with her magic but the way she always treated you. Why would I be mad at you?"

"Because you've always told me witchcraft is dangerous. Helen's dark magic almost ruined our marriage, which means you were right."

"It is dangerous, but whatever Helen was trying to do didn't work, did it? We're still together, and we're happier than we ever have been. It's going to be okay, Piper."

Owen followed Piper and the police officers out of Emily's bedroom, promising to meet them at the police station and declaring his love for his wife. Emily couldn't decide if the scene was romantic or just weird.

Everyone else trailed out behind Owen like some kind of odd parade. Emily hung back, and as soon as the others had disappeared down the hallway, she bent down and grabbed Helen's book. The page Piper had thrown into the toilet was slowly flattening out, but Emily just made a disgusted face and left it there. She would let the police collect that particular piece of evidence.

Knowing it was only a matter of time before Danny would come and take the book to catalog it as evidence, Emily plopped down on her bed and opened it. The brown leather cover was well worn, and the pages inside had occasional smudges on them. Clearly, this was a book Helen had consulted often.

Helen's handwriting was neat and small, and she had written everything in capital letters. The first pages Emily flipped through were spells Helen had copied from other sources: one was noted as being "from Evelyne" and another was attributed to a book called *Secret Spells and Hidden Herbs*. Emily continued turning the pages, and the spells Helen had written down later were obviously her own. Words or entire lines had been crossed out and replaced, and Helen had made notes for herself, recording her attempts to alter details, like the time of day or the phase of the moon when she worked the spell, and whether it had seemed to improve the spell's efficacy.

Despite Piper claiming she had found more sinister spells, all Emily was seeing were the kinds she would expect from someone like Serenity: happiness, career success, and health seemed to be the dominating themes for Helen's spells. Emily thumbed past spells with titles like "To Cure a Cold" and "Money Spell for a Raise at Work."

About halfway through the notebook, the nature of the

spells began to shift. They became more spiteful, and Emily was especially startled to see one called "Crush the Competition." Emily had to wonder if that one had been used to help get Evelyne kicked out as coven leader.

As the spells got darker, Helen had begun writing notes in between them. A glance showed Emily they were full of gossip about the coven and the people Helen had considered her enemies. There were complaints about Serenity being too weak to work really effective magic, a neighbor always growing a prettier garden than Helen, and Abbie being too eager to become coven leader herself.

"So much drama," Emily said out loud.

"Do I need to arrest you for tampering with evidence, too?" Danny was standing in the bedroom doorway, a wry smile on his face.

"I'm not flushing pages, like Piper was," Emily said, feeling slightly embarrassed at having been caught looking through the book. "Unfortunately, Helen's notebook seems to confirm what the other witches have been saying all along: she was into some dark and vengeful stuff, even against her own coven."

"I'm actually looking forward to reading it. If Helen mentions who she was most at odds with, it could help us figure out who our killer is."

Danny had been walking toward Emily as he talked, and he reached out to take the book. Instinctively, Emily's fingers tightened around it, and she pulled it out of his reach. "I have an idea," she said. "What if we leave the book in here? I'll lock my door, so it will be safe."

"Why would you leave it here? We need to know what's in it."

"Because Helen knows better than anyone what's in this book. Rather than us going through it, trying to decide which spell was used against which person, we can ask

Helen to show us what dark magic of hers might have prompted someone to kill her."

Danny frowned and said doubtfully, "You think her ghost could point out a spell that will help us know who might have had the biggest grudge against her. So, for instance, a spell to break up a relationship would point the finger at Piper."

"I see Roger has already filled you in. Yes, that's exactly what I'm thinking."

"I have my doubts about Helen's ghost being able to help us here, but if you want to give this a try, then let's do it. Do you want me to stay while you give Helen her instructions?"

"No, I think she'll be more receptive if it's just me. Call it an instinct."

"Good luck." Danny turned and left, closing the bedroom door behind him.

Once she was alone, Emily stood and placed the notebook on top of her dresser, opening it to what seemed to be about the middle. "Helen Harper, I need your help," Emily called. She continued calling on Helen until she felt a light chill creep up her back, which she took as a sign Helen's ghost was hovering behind her.

"Helen, you don't know who killed you, but you do know who might have suspected you of working dark magic against them. I'm going to leave the room, and while I'm gone, I would appreciate it if you would turn the pages until you find a spell that might help us know who your biggest enemy was. What member of your coven would have had the best reason to kill you? Please, Helen, this would help us so much."

With a resolute nod, Emily left her bedroom, noticing how much warmer the air was in the hallway. She locked the door, then crossed her fingers.

Emily could hear a lot of voices coming from the parlor, and when she walked in, she was surprised to see Trevor, Reed, Trish, Clint, and Sage sitting together. They were all talking excitedly, except for Sage, who had propped her pillow against the side of the wingback chair she was sitting in. Her eyes were closed, though Emily couldn't tell if she was sleeping or simply resting.

"What are you all here for?" Emily asked.

Trish raised her chin proudly. "We're batteries!"

"What?"

"You, Sage, and the witches are going to use our energy to help your ritual tonight," Trish said. "Bringing Scott through the barrier is going to be a team effort."

Emily felt tears starting in her eyes, and she glanced away from Trish's eager face, trying not to cry. She was touched that her friends had come to help, but all she could manage to say was a quiet, "Thank you."

Emily felt a gentle touch on her arm and turned to see Evelyne standing behind her. "Emily, can we please talk? In private?"

"Of course." Emily led Evelyne across the hall to the dining room and shut the door behind them. "What do you want to tell me, Evelyne?"

"I heard the police have Helen's grimoire. They took Piper out in handcuffs, and I'm worried I'll be the next one to get arrested." Evelyne had laced her fingers together tightly.

"Why?"

"We were all waiting at the front of the house when they brought her out, and she shouted at me that there were spells against me in there, too."

Emily nodded. That meant Piper had also seen the spell to bring down the competition and associated it with Evelyne.

"Well, the thing is," Evelyne said, "I was so angry at Helen for getting me kicked out as coven leader, and I was so suspicious that she was working magic against me, that I worked some against her. I wanted her to lose her power and influence, but I took it too far! I never intended for her to die. It's my fault Helen is dead!"

23

"Evelyne!" Emily grasped Evelyne by the shoulders, even as they shook with sobs. "Did you kill Helen?"

Evelyne just cried in answer.

Emily could feel panic rising inside her, and she dropped her hands as she stepped toward the door. "You should tell your story to the police," Emily said.

"I don't want to go to jail!" Evelyne wailed.

"I know, but the best thing you can do right now is cooperate with the police." Emily had her hand on the doorknob. "You stay here. I'll ask Detective Hernandez to come speak to you."

Emily opened the door and sidled out, closing it again behind her.

"Is everything okay in there?" Trevor asked. He had come into the hallway, and he looked searchingly at Emily.

"No. But please guard this door, and do not let Evelyne out. I'm going to get Danny."

Awareness came into Trevor's eyes. "Oh! You got it."

Emily found Danny on the front porch, and she was in such a rush that her words came out as a confused tangle. Danny, at least, seemed to understand part of it, because he ran into the house. By the time Emily caught up, he was already closing the dining room door so he could question Evelyne privately.

Emily went into the parlor and sank onto an open spot on the sofa.

"You think Evelyne killed Helen." Trevor wasn't asking a question.

"She all but admitted it to me just now," Emily said wearily. She fervently hoped Danny would get a quick confession. She was ready to focus on helping Scott, and she was looking forward to falling into bed that night without worrying that she had a murderer sleeping upstairs.

"While they talk, why don't you fill us in on what's been happening with this investigation?" Trish looked excited to get the gossip, and Emily knew she would be sharing it with her customers at Grainy Day Bakery on Monday morning.

Emily gave a brief account of everything from Helen's ghost warning about the dark entity outside the barrier to Piper's unwise attempt to get rid of spells she thought might make her look bad.

Trish whistled when Emily finally finished. "That's a lot. There are plenty of rumors around town about what's going on here, of course, but nothing like that. J.D. Junior came in for a bagel early this morning, and he said the witches actually conducted some kind of magic ritual right there at the funeral home!"

"They did," Emily said, nodding. "It was pretty sedate, actually."

"And here I had pictured them dancing naked in the moonlight," Trish said in mock disappointment.

Sage cracked one eye open. "Nobody will be naked for tonight's rituals, either! At least, I hope not."

"No one will be taking their clothes off inside my cemetery," Emily said firmly.

Clint stood. "I'm going to the kitchen to make coffee. Does anyone want a cup?"

Everyone answered in the affirmative, but Emily noticed that instead of immediately leaving the parlor, Clint went to the rolltop desk first. He grabbed a few sheets of paper and a pen, and Emily turned her head to hide her smile because she didn't want to embarrass Clint. She knew he wasn't really interested in coffee. He wanted to talk to Kelly in private.

"Do you still have that graveyard dirt I gave you from my great-great-grandfather's plot?" Reed asked suddenly.

"I do," Emily answered.

"Good. Take it with you when we go to the cemetery tonight."

"I will." Emily fell silent after that, and her friends followed suit. She closed her eyes and tilted her head back against the sofa. Her brain was sorting through too many worries and details for her to sleep, but it felt good to simply be quiet and still, and she appreciated that her friends seemed to recognize that.

It was the sound of the dining room door opening that prompted Emily to raise her head and look toward the hallway. She had expected to see Danny leading Evelyne out in handcuffs, but instead, it was just Evelyne who walked out. She had a slightly dazed expression, and her red eyes showed that she had been crying some more. With unsteady steps, Evelyne turned and went upstairs.

Danny came into the parlor a few minutes later. He sat in the chair Clint had occupied and sighed. "Evelyne says she did not stab Helen," he announced.

"But she told me it was her fault Helen died," Emily protested.

"She told me the same thing. If she did stab Helen, though, she isn't admitting to it. I think she really believes her magic is what set off the chain of events that led to Helen's murder. She feels guilty."

"We have Piper destroying evidence, Evelyne blaming

herself but not confessing to actual murder, Abbie vying to be coven leader, Malena stealing and then trying to get rid of a knife, and Serenity, who has admitted she was also working magic against Helen."

"And Darlene," Sage said.

"She doesn't count," Emily said quickly.

"That pretty much sums it up, though Darlene stays on the suspect list, too, no matter what her relationship to you is," Danny said. "Unfortunately, we don't have a scrap of evidence against any of them."

"Which means we continue to wait." Trevor looked at Emily. "At some point, you'll have to call the guests who are supposed to be checking in tomorrow and tell them you have to cancel."

"I'm holding out hope this will be taken care of before my next guests arrive," Emily said, though her optimism was swiftly waning.

Clint returned to the parlor with a tray of coffee cups, which he handed around. Emily thanked him profusely as she wrapped her fingers around the warm cup. Since Danny had joined the group, Clint insisted on going back to the kitchen to get coffee for him, too. Danny protested that it wasn't necessary, but Clint was already hurrying down the hallway.

*Teenagers.* Emily smiled to herself, and when Trish shot her a questioning look, Emily gave a little wave. "Clint is one of the best assistants I've ever had, Trish. You raised a good son." Emily wanted to add that he worked hard to keep both the guests and the ghosts at Eternal Rest happy, but she wasn't sure Clint was ready to talk about his burgeoning friendship with Kelly just yet.

Emily heard the sound of the front door, followed by slow footsteps that led into the parlor. "Oh, I didn't realize so many people were here." It was Darlene, and when Emily glanced up, she could see how nervously she was shifting from one foot to the other. "Trish, hi. I haven't seen you in ages."

"Hey, Mrs. B! You need to get over to Oak Hill more often so you can come have my murder biscuits."

Darlene blanched. "I think I've had enough of murder, thank you, but I do need to get to Grainy Day sooner rather than later." Darlene looked at Emily. "Can I talk to you outside?"

"Of course." Emily rose and followed Darlene out onto the front porch. Darlene leaned heavily on the railing, staring out at the trees.

"What's on your mind, Darlene?" After the incidents with Piper and Evelyne, Emily was worried Darlene was about to unload a guilty conscience, too.

"There's something I need to tell you, Emily."

*Oh, no. I was right.*

Darlene's fingers gripped the porch railing, and she swallowed hard before she said, "This entity that killed Scott, it isn't a new presence in his life."

"What do you mean?"

"I mean, those nightmares he was having during his visit to my house, just before his car crash, they weren't new. He had the same dreams when he was a young child. I've been telling myself since his death that the two things weren't related, but knowing what I know now about an entity keeping him captive, I have to admit this thing has been after him since he was a boy."

"What? He never told me about it."

Darlene stared down at her hands. "He never told you, because he didn't remember. That's... That's not all, Emily. When he was just a baby, Scott started showing signs of being a strong psychic medium. Even before he could talk, he would stare at something his dad and I couldn't see, and he would just giggle and babble away. By the time he was three, though, he was seeing dark things, too. He would cry and yell, 'Bad, bad, bad!' It was terrifying. I was just getting into witchcraft back then, and I had met Helen. She told me about the spiritual barrier around Oak Hill and other cities that were special to her coven for one reason or another, and she said that same magic could be used to protect just one person. She introduced me to the rest of the coven, and they helped me enchant a quartz pendant. I gave it to Scott on a necklace, and he stopped seeing ghosts. As he got older, he forgot all of it had ever happened."

"His lucky charm!" Emily exclaimed. "Scott would always wear that when he was stressed out about something. He said it made him feel better."

"He wore it every day as he was growing up. Once he moved to Oak Hill, he was safely inside the barrier, so it didn't matter whether or not he wore it. I don't know what happened on that last visit to my house. Maybe his psychic medium abilities were starting to surface again, or maybe that dark thing had just been waiting around, hoping he'd show up one day without his pendant."

Emily blew out a slow breath. The idea Scott had been a powerful psychic medium—but completely unaware of it —was astonishing. "But if Scott was a medium, shouldn't he have been able to see the ghosts here at Eternal Rest when he wasn't wearing that pendant?"

Darlene finally turned and looked at Emily. "I think maybe all the years of not using his power helped disconnect him from it."

Emily was nodding. "And, back then, we only had two ghosts here: Grandma Gray and the child who sometimes makes their presence known. Neither one is particularly active."

"When he described those nightmares during his last visit, I finally told him about his abilities as a child. He was shocked, but he agreed I had done the right thing in taking steps to protect him."

"You did," Emily agreed. "And now I know why he told me we needed to find a way to protect Eternal Rest spiritually. You told him about the barrier, too, didn't you? He would have known it wouldn't stay strong forever."

"Yes. Unfortunately, me telling him the truth did nothing to keep him safe on his drive home. I think that thing followed him and killed him. Why, I don't know."

"We'll ask Scott when we get him through the barrier tonight." Emily felt like her mind was going to overflow, and she tried to focus on that one thought: Scott was coming home in just a few hours.

Hopefully.

Emily fell silent, and after a few moments, Darlene asked timidly, "Are you mad at me?"

"Mad at you? No, why would I be? You did your best to protect him. He might have been scared by the dark entities as a child, but it sounds like they never tried to harm him."

"No, he never got attacked by anything paranormal. Not until his car crash, at least."

"You did the best you could to protect him, Darlene. You're still trying to protect him." Emily pulled Darlene into a tight hug. She wished Scott had kept that pendant on whenever he went outside the barrier, but he simply hadn't known how important it was. Even Darlene had thought he was safe from his abilities and anything evil that might have wanted to make contact with him. Emily couldn't blame Darlene for Scott's death.

She could, however, blame the dark entity that had caused him to veer off the road and crash. Emily silently vowed she would not only help Scott but also banish the entity responsible for his death. Between Sage, the witches, and even Reed's mysterious knowledge, she was certain she could learn how to do it.

When Emily released Darlene, both women had tears streaming down their cheeks. "Okay," Darlene said, wiping her eyes, "I'm going to sit in the tent and meditate. I need to recharge before the two rituals tonight."

Emily went back into the house and headed straight for the kitchen to get a glass of water. As she walked through the kitchen door, she noticed the paper and pen Clint had taken in there lying on the table.

*Can't breathe. Like when I died but different.*

Emily looked up sadly. "I feel like I can't breathe, either, Kelly."

# 24

Emily said a few reassuring words to Kelly, then turned to get a glass out of the cupboard. She was beginning to open the fridge when she stopped and turned back around. "Kelly, you mentioned a few days ago that you felt like you couldn't breathe. Is it that same feeling again?"

Emily pulled the water pitcher out of the fridge and filled her glass, her back to the kitchen table. When she turned around again, Kelly had written, *Yes. I feel anger. Suffocating.*

"Is the feeling coming from that dark entity keeping Scott trapped outside the barrier?" This time, Emily loaded a few dirty coffee cups into the dishwasher as she waited for Kelly's answer.

*Don't think so,* Kelly had written when Emily looked at the paper again. *The scary thing isn't here.*

"Thank you, Kelly. I know this is helpful information, but I'm not sure yet what it means."

Emily gulped down her glass of water, then went back to the parlor. Only Sage was in there, her head slumped against the pillow and soft, rhythmic snoring telling Emily she was fast asleep. Emily turned and peeked into the dining room, but it was empty, so she quietly went out the front door.

Emily's friends and her guests were all under the tent.

Trevor explained they had silently filed out when they realized Sage was asleep, then he leaned in and said in an undertone, "You look upset."

"Scott's mom shared some surprising news with me," Emily said, just as quietly. "I'm still trying to process all of it."

"You should sit down."

"Yeah." Emily took the empty chair next to Reed and stretched her arms over her head. "I wish I could sleep as soundly as Sage."

"We could hang a hammock in the cemetery," Reed suggested.

Emily couldn't tell if Reed was joking or not. "Don't tempt me. By the way, Kelly just told me she still feels anger and a suffocating feeling. She felt that way a few days ago, too. If only she could tell where the feelings are coming from, I think we might know who killed Helen."

"As you've pointed out, though, most of the coven was angry with Helen," Reed said. "Just because Helen is dead, doesn't mean those feelings toward her have simply disappeared. I wonder if Helen's ghost can sense the anger?"

"I guess we could ask her." Emily jumped up from her chair. "Oh! I totally forgot!"

Reed stood. "Forgot what?"

Emily glanced around to make sure none of her guests were listening in. They were all in a semi-circle on the opposite side of the tent, though, so she said, "I left Helen's notebook in my bedroom and asked Helen to open it up to a page that might give us an idea of who was angry enough to kill her. She had spells in there that look like they were designed to be used against some of the other witches, so I thought maybe she could point us in the right direction. Between Evelyne practically confessing to the murder and Darlene telling me some really surprising things about Scott, I totally forgot I had asked Helen for help."

"What are we waiting for?" Reed asked. He began walking toward the house so quickly Emily had to hurry to catch up to him.

It was only as Reed and Emily were creeping down the hall, trying not to disturb Sage, that Emily realized Trevor and Danny had both followed. Soon, all four of them were crowded around the dresser in Emily's room.

At first, Emily didn't notice any difference in the book. It was still open to about the middle, but at a closer glance, she saw the writing was different than the pages she had selected. Instead of turning to a page of dark magic, though, Helen had flipped the pages to show one of the helpful, positive spells.

Emily sighed. "Helen," she called, "this doesn't help us. I asked you to point out something one of your coven members might have wanted revenge for." On the left page, Helen had made notes about various herbs and their uses. On the right page was a spell called "To Breathe Easy."

Reed bent over and peered closely at the page. "What's the small print at the bottom? It's so tiny I can't read it."

Emily picked up the book and held it just inches from her face. Helen had written in such tiny letters that some of the words were difficult to read. "Not permanent," she read slowly, squinting at the page. "D.M. better at first. Then it came back. They couldn't reach him in time. In the future, refresh spell every six months." Emily dropped the book, which landed on the dresser with a dull thud, and covered her mouth with her hands. "Oh, how awful."

"Helen used this spell on someone, but they later died," Trevor said, sounding both fascinated and horrified. He picked the book up and read, *"Deep and clear, like the waters of a spring, inhale with ease, and shout and sing."*

"Just like the title says, it's a spell to help someone breathe easier," Danny said, looking over Trevor's shoulder. "Maybe it was used on someone who had respiratory problems."

"No wonder Kelly has been saying she can't breathe," Emily said, finally lowering her hands. "This spell was used on someone who had trouble breathing, and Helen thought it had worked, but then that person got worse and died."

"And Helen wrote that they couldn't reach him in time," Trevor said. "Maybe this D.M. person was somewhere remote, and help was too far away."

"If we find out who D.M. was, and how he's connected to the coven, then we might have found our killer," Danny said. "Helen turned to this page to show us there's a witch here who had enough anger and resentment to kill her."

"A life for a life," Reed said quietly.

Emily gasped. "Magic mirror, reflect this evil! That's what the Latin phrase Helen shouted at me translated to. We all thought her ghost was working magic to get revenge on her killer, wanting their fate to be the same as hers. But, maybe, she was trying to tell me that the killer had done to her what she had done to this D.M. A life for a life, like you said, Reed."

"Helen might not be the vengeful spirit we thought she was," Reed said, nodding. "Instead, someone was getting revenge on her."

"Kelly says she feels like she's suffocating," Emily said, reaching out to trace the lines of the spell with a finger. "But the person this spell was used on has died. I doubt their ghost is here, or Kelly and Mrs. Thompson would have sensed it. That must mean one of the witches is somehow channeling that feeling of not being able to breathe."

"Let's go find out which witch it is." Danny's voice was grim, but Emily also caught a tinge of relief in it.

Everyone moved to follow Danny as he headed for the bedroom door, but he turned and put his hands up. "Just Emily, please. We're not a Wild West posse out to catch someone."

Trevor and Reed grumbled but stayed put. As Emily followed Danny out the door, she saw Reed pointing toward her bedroom window and knew they were going to watch the whole scene, anyway.

Danny's hurried pace slowed as he stepped off the porch, and Emily wondered if he was trying to look casual. She trailed a few steps behind, trying to make herself look just as composed but failing miserably.

"Ladies," Danny said as he entered the tent. The five remaining witches all looked up warily. "Helen has indicated to us that there is, in fact, one of you who had more reason than anyone else to want her dead."

Abbie snorted. "Let me guess, you think she was really working dark magic on someone in her own coven?"

"We know she was, but that's irrelevant at the moment. We think she was trying to work positive magic, but it didn't work as well as she had thought, and someone died because of it. Which one of you had a connection to someone with the initials D.M.?"

The witches glanced at each other, but no one spoke. Emily realized Danny wasn't expecting anyone to speak up, anyway, since admitting to a connection would be like admitting to having a motive for murder. He was hoping someone would look uncomfortable or show some other sign of guilt.

"I will question you all again, one at a time, if I have to," Danny continued. "D.M. died because the spell Helen worked on him failed, or so she believed."

Evelyne gave a loud cry. "Just like my magic caused Helen to die!"

Emily felt the tension in the tent rising as the witches continued looking at each other in a mixture of confusion and suspicion. Emily's own chest felt tight with the anticipation, and she told herself, *Take deep breaths. Calm down. Breathe.*

The words in Kelly's notes came back to her. *Can't breathe. Suffocating.* With a start, Emily realized Kelly wasn't the only one who knew what it felt like to not be able to breathe.

"Of course," Emily said quietly, but it was loud enough that Danny turned to her.

"You know who killed Helen," he said without a trace of doubt.

Emily nodded. "I do. At least, I think I do. Trevor even said the spell was probably for someone with respiratory problems. I think D.M. had asthma, which can be a genetic trait. Malena, you were using an inhaler the night Helen died."

Malena jumped up, the folding chair she had been sitting on toppling backward. "He was better after the spell. He didn't need his inhaler for weeks."

"Who is 'he,' Malena?" Danny asked.

"Diego. My brother. It's Helen's fault he died!"

Emily could hear the startled gasps and cries of the others, but it all seemed to come from far away as she focused her attention on Malena. "That day in the cemetery, you told me that we try to protect our loved ones, but we don't always succeed. You asked Helen to work a spell to help your brother, didn't you?"

"It's not my fault he died! It's hers! Helen was the one whose magic wasn't good enough!" Malena's hands curled into fists. "Diego felt so good at first, and he decided to take his boys camping. He swam out to the middle of the

184

lake, and he had an asthma attack. The boys called for help, but he drowned before the ambulance ever arrived."

Malena was crying, and to Emily's surprise, Darlene stood and went over to her, putting her arms around Malena in a hug. "Malena, we knew you had lost your brother, but we didn't know Helen had tried to help him," she said.

"Tried and failed!"

"Helen's knife," Emily said. "You told me you had taken it as a memento, then stashed it in the cemetery because you thought it would make you look guilty. But you actually did use it on Helen, didn't you?"

Malena sobbed loudly and dropped her head onto Darlene's shoulder. "I used mine," she said. "My own dagger. I took Helen's out of her room later that night, like I told you. Then, I dropped my own dagger in the cemetery. I didn't want the police to search my room and find it, because it might have had traces of blood still on it. I told you that story about stealing Helen's dagger, then panicking and throwing it away in the cemetery, so the police wouldn't test it for blood, either. They would never suspect it had been the actual dagger used to, to…"

Malena started sobbing again. Serenity and Evelyne moved close to her, each putting a hand on Malena's back in silent comfort, even though both of the women were crying quietly. Abbie was bent over her knees, her face buried in her hands.

Danny motioned to Darlene, Serenity, and Evelyne, and they stepped back, making room for him to put Malena in handcuffs.

Ten minutes later, Danny and Malena, as well as the officers who had been guarding Eternal Rest, were all gone. Emily sat down in a chair, feeling dazed, and by the faces she saw around her, she assumed everyone else felt the same way. She overheard Trish saying to Darlene, "Bless her heart."

Emily heard the squeak of a window opening, and she looked over to see Sage's face in a parlor window. She yawned and said, "What did I miss?"

It was Abbie who took charge as everyone began to recover from the shock of Malena's confession. No one questioned her authority, but Emily noticed there was a softness in her address that had been missing before. The haughtiness was dampened.

"Helen was my mentor," Abbie said to the other witches, "and I know you all loved her, too, despite her faults. None of us knew Malena was harboring so much resentment and anger. I vow that from now on, I will treat all of you like true sisters. I will share my thoughts and feelings with you, and I will tell you if you've hurt me, so we can make things right. I ask that, in return, you show me the same openness and honesty, so that I can apologize if I have done you harm."

Evelyne, Serenity, and Darlene all nodded, then Abbie looked at the others. "We're down to only four witches for tonight's rituals," she said. "But with all of us, we have ten people who can lend their focus and energy to our magic."

"Fourteen, if you count ghosts," Sage amended. "Mrs. Thompson, Grandma Gray, Kelly, and Helen all want to help, too."

"Fourteen, then." Abbie smiled. "Seven is a powerful number. Two times seven will help us even more. Sisters, new friends, are we ready to bring Scott's spirit through the barrier? The sun hasn't set yet, and we can use its energy to bolster our own."

Everyone agreed enthusiastically, except Emily, who could only nod. The moment had finally arrived, and she realized how important it was that they succeed. She felt a hand in each of hers, and she looked to see Darlene on her left and Sage on her right. "We've got this," Darlene said, though she looked as nervous as Emily felt.

Everyone walked silently into the cemetery and up to the top of the hill. Sage and Emily brought up the rear. Sage occasionally turned around and gestured, and Emily knew she was telling the ghosts of Eternal Rest to follow.

Once they reached the top of the hill, Abbie directed everyone to stand in a semi-circle that was open to the west, where the psychic barrier ran past Hilltop Cemetery. The four witches stood in the center. On their left stood Sage, Emily, and Trevor. Clint, Trish, and Reed stood to their right. Abbie instructed everyone to hold hands, and Sage gave Emily's fingers a reassuring squeeze.

"Sisters, you remember the chant," Abbie said. "For the rest of you, I want you to picture an open doorway in your minds. Put all of your focus and all of your energy into that mental image. It is time to begin. *The barrier stands between you and I…*"

"*But I see a doorway, standing wide,*" chanted Darlene, Serenity, and Evelyne.

Together, the four witches said, "*Our magic created this division, but now we break it with pure intention.*"

Emily squeezed her eyes tightly shut as she pictured a doorway opening up on the horizon and Scott walking through it, his smile wide and his green eyes bright. The witches began the chant again, and Emily started to feel lightheaded. Her knees buckled when the chant was repeated for the third time, and she felt Sage and Trevor let go of her hands to wrap their arms around her, holding her up.

The witches started the chant for the fourth time, but they had only said the first line when Sage shouted, "He's through! Shut it!"

"*Let the doorway close. Our work is done,*" Abbie said immediately. The other witches took up the chant, and they repeated it six more times.

Emily suddenly realized Sage was no longer holding her up. Instead, she was keeping Sage steady. Emily opened her eyes as Sage's head dropped onto Emily's shoulder. "So tired," she whispered. "But the door is closed."

"Where's Scott?" Emily asked, looking anxiously around her.

"The house. He shot right past us and went home. Don't worry, Em. Mrs. Thompson and the others will look after him. Scott and I will both need to recover our energy before we can communicate with each other."

Darlene's eyes were shining with tears, but she was also smiling at their success. Serenity lifted her long skirt and did a little dance of celebration, while Abbie and Evelyne simply looked proud. Everyone walked back to the house, Trevor and Clint supporting Sage. Emily was soon ahead of the rest of them, walking quickly in her eagerness to find her husband.

"Scott?" Emily called as soon as she was through the front door.

There was no answer.

"Mrs. Thompson?"

*Knock.*

"Is Scott with you?"

*Knock.*

"Is he okay?"

Instead of one knock, there was a whole series of them.

The first sounded in the hallway, then the next came from the parlor door. The knocking led Emily to her desk, where Kelly had written, *He's too tired to talk. But we're so happy for you!*

Emily wiped at the tears she felt on her cheeks. She hadn't even realized she was crying. "Thanks. Let him know we're here when he's ready to communicate."

As she sank down into her desk chair, Emily felt light-headed again. The ritual had drained her energy, and it was only her excitement about Scott's ghost finally making it home to Eternal Rest that had gotten her down the hill and back into the house.

It was a few minutes before the others came into the house, and Emily suspected they had intentionally let her have some time alone. By then, Emily had put her head down on the desk.

"I'm going to take a nap in your room," Sage called from the doorway.

"And we're all going upstairs to rest, so we have enough energy for the barrier-strengthening ritual in a couple of hours," Abbie added. "Great work, all of you."

"Thanks," Emily mumbled without looking up.

There were quiet footsteps behind her, and Emily felt arms encircle her in a hug. "I'm so happy we were able to help Scott," Darlene whispered. "I know this is just the first step to giving his spirit peace, but it's a big step."

Emily lifted her head. "Thanks to you and your coven."

After Darlene retreated upstairs, Emily pushed herself up out of her chair. Trevor, Reed, Clint, and Trish were just walking into the parlor. One by one, they gave her a hug, except for Clint, who grabbed a sheet of paper from the desk and left the room. Emily assumed he was going to the kitchen to say goodbye to Kelly.

"Do you want us to stay?" Trevor asked, putting out a hand to steady Emily. "You're clearly exhausted."

"I've got four powerful witches to look after me," Emily said, smiling. "Y'all go on home and try to relax. I know I'm not the only one who's worn out."

Trevor and Reed congratulated Emily on the success of the spell, but Trish said, "Where did Clint wander off to?"

"I think he's in the kitchen," Emily said.

"Teenage boys," Trish grumbled, already beginning to walk out of the room. "They're always hungry."

Emily snickered, but Trish had disappeared in the direction of the kitchen.

By the time Trish called a goodbye as she and Clint left, Emily was sprawled on the sofa, nearly asleep already.

It was dark when Emily woke up, and she opened her eyes to find the four witches staring down at her. "You've been asleep for two hours," Serenity said. "I came in and whispered a spell for good dreams over you. I hope it worked."

Emily sat up and rubbed her eyes. "If I had good dreams, I don't remember them. Is it time?"

Abbie nodded regally. "We're going to the cemetery to strengthen the barrier. Malena's family was from here, you know. It was her grandmother whose coven put the barrier in place around Oak Hill to begin with."

"We've put barriers around a few other towns, too," Evelyne said. "Places where there are people we want to protect."

"It's a shame we couldn't protect Helen," Serenity said sadly.

"Yes, but that was an evil we brought with us. The barriers are in place to keep outside evils at bay. Perhaps there is a lesson in that for us." Abbie looked at the other witches. "Well, sisters, the full moon has risen, and the barrier awaits. I expect Helen is waiting, as well, to help us with the ritual before she moves on to the next stage of her journey. Let us begin."

Emily saw her guests out the door, then headed for the kitchen to make herself dinner. She jumped in surprise when her bedroom door opened. She had forgotten all about Sage.

"Are you feeling better?" Emily asked.

"A bit. You making dinner?"

"Yeah. You're welcome to stay, if you like."

"I'm starving. I'm going to eat with you, and then I'm going to go home and eat dinner with Jen. She should be back from her grandma's in about an hour." Sage sank down into a chair at the kitchen table and yawned. "I might devour a bowl of ice cream, too. I wonder how Scott is doing."

Emily opened the fridge and began to pull out items to make grilled cheese sandwiches. It seemed like a good night for comfort food. "Kelly said he's exhausted, just like you had said. He won't be able to communicate until he's recovered some of his energy."

"Still, Em, I'm really happy for you. And for Scott! He must be so relieved to finally be home."

"I'm relieved, too. Now we just need to help him cross over."

"Well, no one is going anywhere today. I'm sure the other ghosts will let you know when he's recovered." Sage looked up toward the ceiling. "Right, Mrs. Thompson?"

A firm knock sounded from the wall next to the kitchen door. Emily smiled widely, but Sage moaned.

"Sage?" Emily asked worriedly.

"Mrs. Thompson just answered me, which means she's in here with us, but I can't sense her at all!" Sage stared toward the wall opposite her, her forehead creased in concentration. "I can't sense Kelly, or anyone. Em, I think my powers are gone!"

Emily nearly dropped the loaf of bread that was in her hands. "What?"

"My mediumship abilities. They're just gone! I think that ritual for Scott drained more than just my energy. You're going to have to help him, Em. I can't do it anymore."

# A NOTE FROM THE AUTHOR

Thank you so much for reading *Groups Welcome*! The next book, *Quiet Nights*, will wrap up what I have come to think of as The Scott Saga. Buckle up, Readers! It's going to be a wild ride. In the meantime, though, will you please leave a review for this book? As an indie author, reviews mean so much.

Thank you,

*Beth*

# ACKNOWLEDGMENTS

Not only did my test readers help make this book better, but their feedback even improved the next book in the series. Sabrina, Kristine, David, Lisa, and Mom all provided valuable insight. Lia and Nicole polished the manuscript with their expert editing. Thanks to Jena at BookMojo, who keeps me on task and makes sure things are going smoothly behind the scenes.

# NEXT IN THE SERIES

**Find out what's next for Emily, Sage, and the ghosts of Eternal Rest Bed and Breakfast!**

# Quiet Nights

## ETERNAL REST BED AND BREAKFAST BOOK SEVEN
PARANORMAL COZY MYSTERIES

**A new ghost has checked in at Eternal Rest Bed and Breakfast.**

When a high-maintenance celebrity psychic and her reality TV show entourage show up at Eternal Rest Bed and Breakfast, it's the least of Emily Buchanan's worries. A frightening new presence is terrifying her guests and her ghosts.

After a dead body turns up, Emily's best friend, Sage, is the prime suspect. As Sage works to recover her psychic abilities, it's Emily who must communicate with the ghost of the victim to find out who the real killer is.

Along the way, Emily will discover that her guests have a lot of secrets. The biggest secret, though, is what really happened in her late husband's fatal car crash. Emily finally gets the answers she has been seeking, but nothing could have prepared her for the truth...

# BOOKS BY BETH DOLGNER

## The Eternal Rest Bed and Breakfast Series

*Paranormal Cozy Mystery*

Sweet Dreams

Late Checkout

Picture Perfect

Scenic Views

Breakfast Included

Groups Welcome

Quiet Nights

## The Nightmare, Arizona Series

*Paranormal Cozy Mystery*

Homicide at the Haunted House

Drowning at the Diner

Slaying at the Saloon

Murder at the Motel

Poisoning at the Party

Clawing at the Corral

## The Betty Boo, Ghost Hunter Series

*Paranormal Romance*

Ghost of a Threat

Ghost of a Whisper

Ghost of a Memory

Ghost of a Hope

Manifest

*Young Adult Steampunk*

A Talent for Death

*Young Adult Urban Fantasy*

## **Non-Fiction**

Everyday Voodoo

Georgia Spirits and Spectres

# ABOUT THE AUTHOR

Beth Dolgner writes paranormal fiction and nonfiction. Her interest in things that go bump in the night really took off on a trip to Savannah, Georgia, so it's fitting that her first series—Betty Boo, Ghost Hunter—takes place in that spooky city. Beth also writes paranormal nonfiction, including her first book, *Georgia Spirits and Specters*, which is a collection of Georgia ghost stories.

Beth and her husband, Ed, live in Tucson, Arizona. Their Victorian bungalow is possibly haunted, but it's not nearly as exciting as the ghostly activity at Eternal Rest Bed and Breakfast.

Beth also enjoys giving presentations on Victorian death and mourning traditions as well as Victorian Spiritualism. She has been a volunteer at an historic cemetery, a ghost tour guide, and a paranormal investigator. Beth likes to think of it all as research for her books.

Keep up with Beth and sign up for her newsletter at
BethDolgner.com